VENGEANCE

OF

FIRE

ANGELA DUNHAM

DEDICATION

To all the girls still searching for their tribe, don't give up! Your coven is out there, and it's waiting for you.

To all the girls who've lost a mother, I SEE you, and I'm standing by your side. Our hearts may never be the same, but they WILL beat again.

Acknowledgements

My Creative/Editorial Team

Book Covers by Dublin @bookcoversbydublin

Raw Book Editing

To my incredible beta readers ~ thank you for your invaluable feedback and for helping shape this book into what it is today. Your insights and support mean the world to me.

A special thank you to my Mark - your sharp wit and sassy commentary kept me laughing and motivated through this process. You're the very best content editor and I couldn't have done it without you

CONTENTS

PROLOGUE

T*wo Weeks Ago...*

Haven Hargrove balanced on the edge of the lake's muddy shore. Samuel's stern voice echoed in the air, a distant warning, but it was too late. The mirror-like portal beckoned her like a gaping mouth, ready to devour the remnants of her old life and provide her with a new one. All she had to do was jump. Standing on the precipice, she swore she could still hear the faint screams of her friends, still see the fear in their eyes as they faced off against an unimaginable evil. Biting back the tears, she cursed at the unfairness of it all. The portal before her undulated as if to say tick-tock, times almost up. The floating sphere was a rip in the fabric of existence that simultaneously revealed two realities to her. On her side of the portal, she stood on the rain-slicked bank of a lake in Cassadaga, Florida, while the other side of the gateway provided her with a view of a lush, sun-drenched forest. The verdant-colored landscape called to her like a lover, promising answers to all the questions her heart yearned to find. The pull was strong, and Haven was tired of fighting for everyone else and losing the people she loved in the process. It was time to put herself first. Samuel called out for her again, but her determination drowned out his words, and with one defiant leap, she plunged into the unknown.

Her stomach somersaulted as the portal flipped her upside down and spat her out on the other side. The landing was anything but graceful, and she grunted as a pinch of pain ran up her right side. Staring up through the opening she'd just come through, she saw the raw panic inside Samuel's onyx-colored eyes as he gaped down at her from the other side. Then, before she could blink, the gateway shrank down to the size of a pinpoint before vanishing completely. Exhausted, she sat on the cold, hard ground to take in her new surroundings. Shivering, she wrapped her arms around herself to try and keep warm. This land was where her mother was born; her soul was sure of it, but geographically speaking, she had no idea where she was. Studying the lush forest that encompassed her, she noted the differences in the trees and landscape, but this wasn't Florida or her hometown of Colorado, so where in the hell was she? Depictions of the small village where her mother grew up flashed through her mind like a snapshot of the past, but nothing remained. There was only a large empty clearing and the dense forest beyond.

The frigid air was relentless as it blew gusts of icy wind against her exposed skin. If push came to shove, she could use her fire magic to keep herself warm, but since she was so exhausted, the longevity of her magic was questionable. Closing her eyes, she used all her witchy senses to tune into the world around her, and in the quiet, she heard alight trickling noise off to her right that indicated a water source was somewhere nearby, but there were no sounds of cars or people. There was only the peaceful hum of nature. The silence was soothing but also a testament to how alone and removed she really was. Taking a deep breath, she opened her eyes and tried to appreciate the raw beauty of the forest, but the haunting memories of her mother's last days in this place were too much for her to bear. All signs pointed to her mother being dead, but something deep inside of her refused to believe that, and that was the real reason she'd jumped. She needed answers, answers only this place could provide.

Pushing herself off the ground, she felt the earth vibrate under her palms as a flood of dark magic surged up from the dirt and seeped its way into her body. Her back bowed and sweat broke out across her brow as she fought for control. The insidious magic wanted to use her, to control her, but some rational part of her brain screamed *NO!* Dropping to her knees, she tried to calm her racing heart as the power vacated her body as quickly as it had come on. Taking a few deep, choppy breaths, she stared over at the unassuming clearing, wondering what in the hell she'd just been exposed to. This deceptive place held a lifetime's worth of secrets, and she had no intention of moving on until she uncovered them all. Squaring her shoulders, she stood on shaky legs and said goodbye to her old life as she headed into the forest to embrace her new one.

Present Day ...

As Haven ran toward the back door, she could already hear their screams. She was too late, and the words of the fatal spell echoed inside her ears like she'd been the one who cast it herself.

I have emptiness in a glass

An emptiness like the one I feel

Once the object returns to me

My emptiness will heal

That spell had been the downfall of them all. Barreling inside the house, Haven tripped over the legs of a young blonde girl who was slumped over in the corner, bleeding from a head wound. Stopping briefly to check her pulse, she breathed in a sigh of relief when she realized the girl was still alive. The same couldn't be said for the teenage girl with a severed neck or the dead woman inside the pantry whose stomach had been sliced wide open. The monster responsible for their deaths looked exactly like the dead woman inside the pantry, but she saw the real evil lurking under the surface. The beast had a satisfied grin plastered across its face as it choked a red-haired girl in its tight grip, and amid its bloodlust, it didn't notice her approach until it was too late.

Blasting it with a ball of fire, the monster shrieked in outrage as it dropped the half-conscious girl to the ground. The beast stared in disbelief at the burn mark on its chest before it morphed into the real version of itself. The evil entity before her looked alienlike now, with elongated spindly limbs and grey-colored skin. It was a sight nightmares were made of.

Squaring its shoulders, it stretched to its full height before pegging her with a menacing stare. "Isn't this an interesting turn of events? I'll enjoy stealing your powers as well."

Her psychic abilities told her the creature was a doppelgänger, but she'd never faced one before and had no idea what she was up against. Blasting it with another wave of her fire, she was horrified when the creature's body absorbed the flames.

"Nice try, you stupid witch, but fire doesn't work on my kind."

Panicking, Haven did the only thing she could think of and made up a banishing spell on the fly. Thinking up the words as she went, she prayed the spell worked.

Beast of shadow, I bind your might

By blood and fire and cleansing light

Return to darkness, where you belong

Your time is over; your power is gone

The doppelgänger stretched out a claw-tipped hand toward her, and just before it made contact, its body blinked out of existence. She had no idea where she'd sent the beast, but that was a worry for another day. Right now, she had one hell of a magical mess to try and fix.

Turning to face the broken girl who'd summoned her, she was relieved to find her still alive. "Hello, cousin. I got your message."

CHAPTER I

As Haven sped through the deep woods with her unexpected passenger, she tried to take solace in the fact that she'd finally found a member of her family. Even if the girl sitting beside her hadn't been the one she'd been hoping for. Her cousin, Sarin, had dabbled in some serious spell casting without any experience and accidentally created a doppelgänger as a by-product of an *I don't know what the fuck I'm doing* excuse for magic wielding. In Sarin's defense, the spell had successfully called blood to blood by summoning her, but the other girls in Sarin's makeshift coven had failed to close the circle properly, and when she found them, the doppelgänger had already killed Sarin's mother, and another young witch named Selene.

Pushing the car to its limit, she sped through the winding forest road toward the cabin. Time wasn't on their side, and Sarin desperately needed a crash course in Witchcraft, along with some medical attention. The girl's arm was a bloody mess, even with the makeshift tourniquet wrapped around it. Out of the corner of her eye, she watched Sarin's fingers flex as her cousin gripped the strap of her seatbelt. She knew she was driving like an asshole, but this was a matter of life and death. Selene's distraught aunt and crazy-ass coven leader was on the hunt for Sarin. The witch blamed Sarin for Selene's death, and from what Haven had been told, there was no talking sense into that crazy bitch, or crazy witch in this scenario. Speeding around a sharp turn in the road, the car banked too far to the left, and Haven had to swerve to avoid a head-on collision with an oncoming semi.

"Shit, Haven, that was close!" Sarin cursed.

Haven slowed down, but only slightly. "I don't want your blood on my hands."

"Then stop diving like a maniac. If we get in a car accident and I die before the coven finds me, then this is all for nothing!"

True, she thought, but the day's horrible events were still fresh inside her mind, and all she wanted was to get her cousin to a safe place. Walking in the backdoor of Sarin's house earlier that day had been traumatic, to say the least, and it was going to take a lifetime's worth of therapy to erase all the blood and gore from her memory bank.

Sarin eased her grip as the road flattened out in front of them. "How much longer will it take to get there?"

"We're close. I just wish this piece of shit beater car could go faster."

"Any faster, and this tin can is going to explode," Sarin commented as she pulled her cell phone out of the small duffle bag she'd packed on the fly.

"What are you doing with that? I thought I told you only to bring the essentials!"

"In what universe is a cell phone not essential?" Sarin quipped.

"In the universe where cell phones can be tracked. Turn it off!" Haven snapped. She didn't mean for the statement to come out as harsh as it had, but now wasn't the time for hand-holding.

Sarin stared down at her phone but didn't move. The girl was clearly in shock.

Reminding herself that this girl had just experienced a significant loss, she tried to temper her response. "I'm not mad, but we have to be careful. I don't think you're thinking clearly, which is completely understandable considering what you just went through, but I need you to turn it off. Okay?"

Sarin clicked a few buttons before letting the phone drop into her lap.

Resting her head back on the headrest, she asked, "How much of a head start do you think we have?"

Haven didn't have a good answer for that, but she knew they were both in some deep shit. Aside from the threat of the coven, the doppelgänger would be looking for revenge on Sarin and on her for banishing it. Since she'd never encountered one of its kind before, she had no idea how long her banishment spell would last or how far away it had sent the nightmarish creature. Taking Sarin out of town seemed like the only way to ensure her odds of surviving. Haven was renting a remote cabin close to the clearing, and it seemed like the safest option for the time being. It was already spelled to protect against basic intruders, but now she needed to add a cloaking spell to ward it against magic users. It was the only way she could successfully hide them from the coven. Whether it would work against the doppelgänger remained to be seen. Sarin had been quiet and withdrawn most of the drive, and she understood why. It wasn't every day you lost two people you loved at the hands of a monster. Now wasn't the right time to discuss all the horrors Haven had seen and experienced in this world, not when Sarin had just been exposed to her first visceral taste of it, but maybe someday, she could be a sounding board for her.

"It's hard to gauge how quickly the coven might find us without knowing what powers they wield or how advanced their magic is. Can you tell me anything about them?"

Sarin's harsh scowl was telling. "No. I'm close with Faith, but her mother never liked me, and we weren't on good terms before Selene died. Until today, I had no idea she even had a so-called coven. I don't think Faith knew about it, either. All her mother did was lie and try to stop us from practicing magic and look how well that turned out."

The last word came out on a strangled cry, and Sarin broke down. "This can't be real. My Mom? Selene? They can't be gone, right?"

Haven wanted to comfort her, to tell her they were in a better place, but she didn't know if such a place existed. She knew that souls moved on after death, but she also knew they were lost to us while we were on this side of the veil.

"You're a spirit witch, Sarin, so you know we're made up of more than our bodies. Hold on to that right now. Hold on to the notion that you might see them again when it's your turn. I know that doesn't stop the hurt, but it's something."

"That's a nice dream." Sarin said absently, "But it doesn't take away my grief. Or the heart-wrenching reality that I'll never get to talk to my mom again. How does someone even begin to cope with that on any level?"

"By surviving!" Haven responded sternly.

"Your Mom wouldn't want anything bad to happen to you, and she wouldn't want you to blame yourself for her death. If you can't do it for yourself, do it for her because no matter where she is, she isn't ready for you to join her. Channel your anger and your grief and turn it into whatever it is that you need to push through this with me. Once we're safe, you can have the breakdown, but right now, I need you to get your shit together and try to recall any important information about that family!"

The harsh words seemed to reach some part of Sarin's rational brain, and after dabbing her eyes a few times, her cousin managed to pull back the tears. "I never asked Faith what her mom's powers were. It was all very hush-hush in that family, and it felt like an invasion of privacy to probe my best friend. Faith's Mom has a twin sister named Fallon, and her daughters are Phoebe and Selene, but aside from them, I don't know anyone else in their family or coven."

Sarin paused, her eyes welling up again. "Before Selene died, she and Phoebe hadn't manifested any active powers yet, and Faith had a theory it was Farrow's doing. Faith is a fire witch, but the power is new. She just discovered it when she saved me from the doppelgänger the first time."

"Then we're going in blind," she said as she willed the car to go faster. "The cloaking spell should buy us time, but I'll have to research my grimoire to find any other spells that might be useful."

"I don't know if I thanked you yet," Sarin said absently. "If you hadn't come when you did, Faith and I would be dead too."

"We got lucky with the timing, and I wouldn't have been there at all had you not cast the summoning spell. When it comes to magic, there's always a price, Sarin, and I'm very sorry the cost of finding me meant losing your loved ones."

"If it hadn't been that spell, it would have been something else. I was so hell-bent on figuring out how to use magic that I lost sight of what was important. I was reckless, and it cost me everything," Sarin admitted on a shaky breath.

She placed her free hand on top of Sarin's as she pulled the car off the back road and onto the gravel-filled street that led to the cabin. "I'll teach you, Sarin, and I'll make sure you never feel reckless with magic ever again."

Sarin sniffled as the car stopped just outside the tiny A-framed cabin. It was quaint and painted in a dark green hue that helped it blend in with the forest around it. Haven had chosen it for its proximity to the clearing, but now, it would serve as the perfect hiding place for Sarin once she cast their magical camouflage.

"Grab your bag, and let's get inside. Faith's seen my real face, and it will be too easy to spot two read heads if we don't do something about it."

"You can trust Faith. She's not like her mother."

She rolled her eyes at her cousin's naiveté. The girl still had a lot to learn. "I don't trust anyone when it comes to magic and power, and you shouldn't either."

Anger colored Sarin's features as she followed her toward the front door of the cabin. "Faith is the only person in this world that I do trust, and if I use your same logic, then I shouldn't trust you either."

Flashing her cousin a coy smile, Haven unlocked the door to the cabin, "Now you're getting it."

CHAPTER 2

"There's only one bedroom, so I hope the couch is okay. I wasn't expecting company when I rented this place," Haven announced as she watched Sarin take in their modest accommodations.

The cabin had been updated per the listing on Airbnb, but she was pretty sure all that meant was newish plumbing and a fresh exterior paint job. The inside was a remnant of the '70s, with oak laminate cabinets and vinyl floor tiles that were probably full of asbestos.

"It is what it is," Sarin replied flatly as she dumped her duffle bag on the worn carpet like it was nothing but trash.

Haven felt the urge to hug her but refrained; they weren't there yet. Pivoting, she headed into the pocket-sized bedroom to retrieve her mother's grimoire. Pulling it out of its glamoured hiding place in the bottom drawer of the nightstand, Haven ran her fingers over the embossed symbol of the triangle that decorated its cover. It represented the elemental magic she shared with her mother and her rich Wiccan heritage. Cradling the book like the precious possession it was, Haven headed back into the living room and gently placed it on the glass coffee table.

Taking a seat on the plaid threadbare sofa, she gestured for Sarin to join her, "Sit, please."

Sarin's eyes were glued to the old, worn book as she sat beside her. The rickety frame of the worn couch let out a loud groan under their combined weight, and when she opened the thick bound cover to look for the spell she needed, she saw Sarin's eyes widen.

"I can feel the power pulsing from it. It's making my heart race."

That was curious, she thought.

"You can touch it if you want to," she urged her cousin, wanting to test out a theory.

Sarin reached out with a trembling hand, and when her finger brushed the edge of the book, she yanked them back lightning fast. "Ow! The stupid thing shocked me!"

"Well, that settles that!"

"Settles what?" Sarin asked with skepticism. "That the book hates me? And how is that even possible? Is it alive or something?"

"It means the opposite, actually. It initially shocked me, too, but as you learn to use your powers, the severity of its effects should fade. It's not alive, per se, but since it holds a lifetime's worth of magic, it has power, or maybe it has power because it holds so many spells? I don't know if the shocks are a test of resilience or recognition, but it's only ever shocked the two of us. I'm not an expert on the mechanics of my mother's spell book. Or any spell book for that matter."

"What are you an expert on, then?" Sarin snapped.

The scathing tone in her cousin's voice took Haven aback. "Apparently, I'm an expert at saving your ass. Look, I get it. You're angry, sad, and grieving, and regardless of our shared genes, I'm just a stranger to you. But here's a fun fact - I didn't ask to get caught in the middle of all your magical bullshit, so if you don't want my help, there's the door! Otherwise, I need you to understand that we're under a real-time crunch here, and I don't need this kind of pushback when I'm just trying to help you!"

Sarin glanced at the door and then back to her before letting out a defeated sigh. "I don't know where that came from. I do want your help, but everything feels so wrong. I feel like the entire world flipped upside down this morning, and now I'm just over here living inside an episode of *Stranger Things*."

Her heart constricted under her cousin's words. Sarin had no idea just how spot-on she was. Maybe her theory about slow-rolling the truth of the universe was wrong. Maybe her cousin could handle more than she was giving her credit for. Then again, Sarin had been wounded on a fundamental level and deserved some time to process her new existence before they did a deep dive into the shitshow that was the cosmos. The angry outbursts were understandable, and if Haven was being honest with herself, she didn't know anything about the girl other than the fact that they shared a few strands of DNA. For all she knew, Sarin could turn out to be a very real and very volatile threat. With all that pent-up angst, the girl was a ticking time bomb full of untrained magic. The only advice Haven could give her was a lesson she'd had to learn for herself the hard way.

"One day, you'll wake up, and it won't hurt so much. That's the only solace I can give you. In my experience, time is the only thing that can heal a broken heart. And even then, the pain never really leaves you; it just dulls to a manageable throb you carry with you forever. I can help you get that time, Sarin, but first, we need to find the right spell."

She was surprised when she felt the wet stain of a tear roll down her cheek. It wasn't like her to get emotional, but the last few weeks had been a lot. Staring into a set of green eyes that were so similar to her own, Haven felt the connection click into place when Sarin reached out and gently wiped away her tears. This scared, wounded girl beside her was her family, and she would do everything in her power to help keep her safe. Sarin must have felt it, too, because her eyes softened briefly before her wall of emotion burst wide open.

"Thank you for the kind words. I'm not sure I deserve them right now, but thank you. I have so many intrusive thoughts spiraling inside my head right now, and it feels hard to concentrate. What happens after this, Haven? I mean, did I really just leave my mother's dead body in the pantry of our home for anyone to find? Won't the police be looking for me? God, how the fuck did I end up here?"

Sucking in a harsh breath, Sarin continued with her panic-filled rant. "I know Fallon will take care of Selene, but what if Farrow makes her leave my mom there all alone? I can't even deal with that. I think I have to go back! I need to go back!"

"Breathe, Sarin. Just breathe. I think you're having a panic attack."

Sarin dropped her head into her hands and finally let it all go. Pulling her in close, Haven held her until Sarin's chest stopped heaving.

"After we cast the spell, and I'm convinced they can't track you, you should call Faith. Maybe she can put your mind at ease and help answer some of these questions."

Nodding, Sarin wiped her nose on the back of her sleeve.

Refocusing on the time-sensitive task, Haven pulled the ancient grimoire into her lap and asked it to find the spell they needed. The pages moved on their own accord, creating a tiny breeze inside the room as the ancient tome searched its interior at her request.

She felt Sarin go rigid beside her. "It's okay. It's supposed to do that."

"You'd think I'd be used to seeing magic by now, but every time I witness it, it still takes my breath away," Sarin stated with reverence.

She understood that. Every time she practiced, it felt like a piece of her soul was being fed. Magic was beautiful and pure and a fundamental part of who they were. The book's pages slowed down before stopping on a threadbare page about two-thirds of the way in. The cloaking spell it illuminated was familiar to Haven but not one she'd put to memory. It called for a small amount of blood and some salt to cast the circle. Reaching under the couch, she pulled the salt container out from one of the many magical supply bins she had stashed around the cabin.

Handing it to Sarin, she asked, "Can you cast the circle for me?"

Sarin took what was offered and dutifully surrounded the open area of the living room with a wide ring of sea salt. Stepping inside the circle, Sarin waited quietly while Haven grabbed a small bowl and athame from her kit. Joining her cousin, Haven then used the ceremonial knife to slice a deep gash across the center of her palm. Holding her hand over the bowl, she squeezed the wound until several drops of her blood landed inside the bowl. Handing the knife to Sarin, she motioned for her to do the same.

Sarin winced as she scored her own hand, and once their blood mixed inside the bowl, Haven reached for her.

"Take my hand and repeat these words three times."

Wanted by others, dark as night

I cloak us now in the evening light

To give us time to stay or fight

We ask to be hidden from enemies sight

A soft wind blew through the space as Sarin's voice blended in with hers, and she shuddered under the weight of their combined power. Casting with Sarin made the magic feel bigger somehow, and when the spell was complete, she felt the familiar warmth wash over her, which signified the spell was a success.

"Did it work?" Sarin asked as she rested her head against one of the couch cushions.

She took note of the dark circles under her cousin's eyes. The girl had to be exhausted after all she'd endured.

"I think it did. Why don't you take the bed tonight? You look like you could use a good night's sleep."

Sarin responded with a soft snore. Pulling one of the thick wool blankets from the basket on the side of the couch, Haven draped it over her. The girl was so drained that she'd fallen asleep sitting up. Haven knew the awkward angle was going to give her a major neck kink in the morning, but she refused to disturb her. Mouthing the words to a simple relaxation charm, she hoped the added magic would help her cousin get a night of peaceful sleep. Curling up on the other end of the couch, Haven closed her own eyes, praying she could deliver on her promise of keeping Sarin safe.

CHAPTER 3

The wind blew violently, whipping Haven's hair around her face as she stood before The Devil's Chair and the obscenely handsome man who occupied it. The scene before her looked precisely as it had the last time she'd been in Cassadaga. A few weeks ago, she'd been sent here to try and stop one of three Hell gates from opening and, by default, jump-starting the apocalypse. The plan had been complicated: defeat the guardian of the Hell gate called The Mirror of Retribution and deliver a mystical bomb to Heaven with the help of Lucifer himself. Against all odds, she'd succeeded in doing both, but the guardian had been formidable, bringing her to the brink of death. In a desperate bid to save herself, Haven had siphoned too much power from The Devil's Chair, inadvertently binding herself to Lucifer in the process. Lucifer couldn't walk Earthside, but she'd found a loophole by using her magic to call him to The Devil's Chair. The consequences of that choice had yet to come to fruition, but she had a bad feeling they were on the horizon. The chair was ancient and had a deceiving facade that hid the immensity of its true power, just like Lucifer himself. Legend said that anyone who sat in The Devil's Chair could call upon Lucifer, and the fallen angel would be forced to respond. That idea was laughable. If Lucifer didn't want to communicate with you, you were shit out of luck. But as fate would have it, he'd had no qualms about spilling the tea with her since day one.

Speaking of the infuriating king of Hell, that asshole was busy smirking over at her, looking all innocent schoolboy with a crush rather than the epitome of all evil. In all his tall, dark glory, Lucifer managed to look both regal and smug as he lounged in the red brick chair. His wavy jet-black hair framed his all-too-perfect face, and his onyx-colored eyes were tinged with a bright ring of red. The crimson halo was the only indication of the true beast lying in wait. His hooded gaze lingered on her. It was assessing and felt oddly intimate. His posture was casual, but Haven knew from past experience that nothing with this man or monster was easy breezy.

Crossing his arms over his broad chest, he slowly looked her up and down. "I have to say, I didn't anticipate that little nosedive of yours into the portal. You get increasingly intriguing by the day, don't you?"

She wasn't sure if she wanted to blush or vomit. The polarizing feeling was a constant annoyance whenever he was around.

"I have that effect on people," he said with a wink, clearly reading her thoughts.

"And maybe you didn't defeat all your wantonness after all. Should I summon the deceased guardian back from my realm to give you another go?"

She felt slightly embarrassed at his mention of the sin she'd had to overcome to defeat the guardian. Since Hell had been made for sinners, one of the caveats for keeping it at bay had been for her to face up to her own. But that chapter of her life was over, and she had no interest in reliving it. Owning your shit was tough, even if the payoff meant saving the world. The comment was a low blow, even for him, and now, all she wanted to do was punch him in his stupid, handsome face.

Trying to keep her voice as casual as possible, she asked, "Why am I here? I thought we were done?"

"I believe the last words I said to you were, I have big plans for you, which would imply that we are very much not done!"

The devilish smile that bloomed across his face made her blood run cold.

"What could you possibly want from me?" she spat through clenched teeth.

Lucifer all but purred as he looked over her with a mix of malice and what appeared to be lust. "So many things, my little Witch. But for starters, show me your hand."

The brand on her palm burned in response to his command. Was this some kind of test? What if she didn't want to play this game? Could she deny him?

"I could force you," he warned, a tinge of anger coloring his voice. "Or you could just comply."

A wash of his dark energy threatened to buckle her knees. Holding her hand, palm up, she showed him what he wanted to see. The raised black and red scar that marred the center of her palm looked similar to a triquetra made from three intertwining sixes. The gruesome brand was a daily reminder of what she'd lost and what she'd bargained away without her knowledge to keep herself alive. Usually, she kept it hidden with a glamour spell, but if he wanted to see it so badly, then so be it.

"My mark looks good on you!" he declared in a provocative voice that made her skin crawl.

She didn't like the possessive, predatory look in his eyes. "Why did you do it? Mark me, I mean? I thought all you wanted was to stick it to God. I did my part and helped you with the spell, so why involve me any further?"

"We all make choices. When you harnessed my power through the chair to stop the guardian, you made yours."

"How could I make a choice I didn't know I was making?"

His look of disappointment was palpable. "Semantics aside, we are now intertwined. Your powers will grow thanks to my mark, and when I call on you again, be ready."

"Be ready for what?" she screamed, but Lucifer had already disappeared, leaving his crumbling ancient chair empty.

The scene around her began to blur as her consciousness was pulled back to the real world. Sitting up on the couch, she was covered in sweat and felt disoriented over what had just gone down. Had it been a dream? Or had Lucifer really come to her somehow? The mark on her palm still burned, and when she turned it over, she gaped at the sight of her scar. The raised outline now pulsed with an eerie red light that looked frighteningly similar to the red rim around Lucifer's obsidian-filled eyes. Haven didn't know what Lucifer wanted from her, but no matter what it was - it couldn't be good.

CHAPTER 4

Haven woke up in a foul mood. Her back was sore from sleeping on the cramped couch, and the brand on her hand was throbbing with its new and improved ring of fire. The stupid thing was like her own personal scarlet letter. Slowly maneuvering herself off the couch, she tiptoed into her bedroom. Sarin was still dead to the world, and Haven didn't want to wake her, not when her head was still spinning. All of Lucifer's cryptic bullshit had her feeling like a caged animal. She was done being a pawn for all these self-righteous, powerful beings, and if he thought for one second that she'd let him use her, he was sorely mistaken. Her top priorities were keeping Sarin safe and figuring out what was happening inside that clearing. Lucifer and all his esoteric bullshit could suck it. He had a way of getting under her skin, and the fact that she let him just pissed her off even more. Standing at the edge of her bed, she blanked. She'd come in here to do something, but what the hell was it? The room was spotless, and unless she wanted to unmake and remake her bed, there was nothing else to clean. Pacing around the room to try and calm her nerves, she tried and failed to erase the image of Lucifer's handsome face from her mind. She didn't want to be tied to anyone, especially not the very sexy and very volatile ruler of Hell. Nope, not today, Satan!

For right now, she was choosing to believe that their encounter had been nothing more than a dream, and two, that the new blazing red ring in the center of her palm was just a strange coincidence. That train of thought was naive, but she already had ninety-nine problems, and Lucifer didn't need to be one of them. Her cell phone chose that moment to buzz on its charging station, and she was thankful for the distraction. Glancing over at the brightly lit screen, she felt her stomach drop when she realized who it was. After fourteen days of avoidance, she'd become an expert at ghosting her father. She'd sent him a text to let him know she was alive and safe, but other than that, she'd been avoiding him like the plague. She knew she couldn't escape his wrath forever; she owed him more than that. And now that Sarin was somewhat safe inside the cabin, it felt like the right time to slap a much-needed Band-Aid on the bad situation. For better or worse, she needed to make peace with her dad before anything else in her life went to shit. She could do it. She had to do it. Memories of leaving him flooded her mind with a fresh wave of guilt. Her father, Ryan, with his huge heart, had voiced his desire to help her and her friends close the gates of Hell. But subjecting her very human father to a magical fight with a mythical guardian was too dangerous. Ultimately, her choice to leave him behind had cost her his trust, and now, the guilt clung to her like a shadow of shame.

Taking a deep breath, Haven centered herself and mouthed the words to a spell she knew like the back of her hand. It was an astral projection charm that would whisk her soul to wherever she wished. She considered calling her dad back first, but that wasn't good enough. Deep in her heart, she knew her apology needed to happen face-to-face. Feeling her soul move through the ether, she kept her proverbial fingers crossed that her dad would be willing to have the hard conversation. Reappearing inside the outdated kitchen of her childhood home, Haven was overwhelmed by all the familiar sights and smells. The sink was overflowing with dishes, and a thick layer of dust coated everything in sight. In the past, she'd taken care of most of the housework, and without her around, it appeared all the things had piled up. Cue more regret with a side of shame. Sighing, Haven left the mess and walked into the living room to find her father sprawled on the weathered leather sofa, watching the news. He had deep lines etched on his handsome face, and the regret inside her swelled to a breaking point when she noticed the drink in his hand. He never drank.

"Dad?" she called out tentatively, trying her best not to startle him.

Jumping up, he spilled his drink. So much for not scaring him. "Shit! Ruby Red!"

Their eyes met, and then he was rushing toward her. Reaching out, he tried to pull her in for a hug, but when his hand ghosted through her non-corporal form, he stepped back and shook his head in disappointment.

"Couldn't even show up for real, huh? Why am I not surprised?"

"Harsh!" she snapped. She hadn't expected a welcome home party, but his disdain for her was palpable.

"What did you expect? You've been gone for weeks," he stated with a shrug.

She wanted to argue with him, but he was right. She deserved his anger for leaving him. It was exactly what her mother had done. But now, she understood her mother's position. Sometimes, you had to leave the ones you loved to protect them. Too bad he didn't see it that way. Clearing her throat, she tried to remember all the things she'd come here to stay, but it was hard to concentrate under his unrelenting glare. Growing up, she'd always hated upsetting him, and now, standing in front of him like this, she felt five years old again.

"You don't know what it was like...." she paused, struggling to find her big girl voice.

"You're right, I don't know!" he all but spat. "And why don't I know? Because you cast a sleeping spell on me! How dare you! I told you I wanted to help, and instead, you put me on the sideline without my permission."

"You're human!" she yelled in an equally heated voice. "You have no idea what it's like to have all these powers and no one to guide you. I jumped in and helped my friends because I had no choice. I know you wanted to do something, but if you had come, you'd be dead right now, and I would've been too distracted with grief to defeat the guardian. I did what I had to do to protect you and the rest of the world, and I don't care if you can't see that."

Tears began to roll down her face in hot streaks. "Don't you get it? I lost mom! I can't lose you too!"

At the sight of her tears, her dad's expression softened. "You're right, Haven. I don't understand any of it. Especially the part where you disappeared *after* you won."

His words cut like a knife. "Once the guardian was gone, the portal it came through stayed open and showed me the clearing where Mom's coven used to live. It called to me, Dad. It felt like she called to me. How could I ignore that?"

Her father's eyes shot wide with disbelief. "Do you really think she might be alive after all this time?"

"Honestly, I don't know. But something inside that clearing called to me, and I need to see it through."

Staring into his warm, optimistic eyes, she felt a ping of regret for telling him. She didn't want to get his hopes up. If her mother was still alive, there was no telling what kind of person she might be today or if she had any interest in reconnecting with her estranged family.

"I won't ask you to give up on your mother. God knows I never have, but I need you to check in with me from here on out. No more disappearing! Agreed?"

She nodded. It was the least she could do. "And Dad, there's one more thing. Did mom ever tell you about a brother?"

"No, but I didn't ask a lot of questions about her family when we were together. It was a touchy subject."

Touchy was putting it mildly, Haven thought.

"It's a long story, but I have a cousin from mom's side of the family. Her name is Sarin, and her dad died around the time mom's coven went to MIA, so I was curious if she ever mentioned him. When this is all said and done, I'd like you to meet her."

"Haven, are you sure you should be associating with her? I'm not sure it's a good idea after what your mom told me about her coven. What if she's a decoy sent by the coven to flush you out?"

She hadn't considered that possibility, but she didn't think Sarin was a threat. "My ESP is telling me to trust her, and I always listen to my gut."

"If she's not a threat, she'll always be welcome in this house."

Her eyes misted over as she felt the familiar pull that signaled her time in the astral plane was ending. "There's so much more I want to tell you, but I have to go."

"Remember your promise, Ruby Red."

"I love you, Dad! If Mom is still alive, I promise I'll find her."

The image of her dad's loving face disappeared as her soul was transported back to her waiting body. The merge between body and soul was always the most uncomfortable part of the experience. Her essence was fluid and free in her non-corporeal form, but now, trapped inside her own skin, it felt heavy and claustrophobic. The trapped, panicky feeling would pass in time, but the more she astral projected, the longer it took her to shake it off. Stretching out her limbs, she smiled for the first time in a long time. She still had a lot of work to do to make things right with her father, but for today, they were okay, and that was a win.

CHAPTER 5

Faith Bradbury stood hand in hand with her cousin Phoebe as they watched the cemetery staff lower Selene's casket into the large rectangular-shaped hole in the dirt. This was the second burial of the day, and when Phoebe trembled, Faith squeezed her hand in a show of solidarity and compassion. The loss of her young cousin was enough to bring her to her knees, but Faith knew it was so much worse for Phoebe. Selene had been her twin, and Faith couldn't imagine what was going on inside Phoebe's head as she watched her other half be laid to rest. Staring over at the second plot that had yet to be filled in, Faith felt a fresh wave of sorrow wash over her. Sarin should be here. Burying your best friend's mother without said best friend in attendance was wrong on so many levels, but it was the least she could do.

Farrow's hatred for Sarin ran deep, and if she'd gotten her way, Lynne's body would have stayed inside the pantry to rot. Luckily, her aunt Fallon had stepped up and talked some sense into her deranged sister, which was a testament to Fallon's strength and resilience since she'd just lost one of her daughters. After the attack, Fallon had gone into fix-it mode and cast some serious magical Houdini on the cops who'd shown up to interview them. Faith had no idea what lies Fallon had fed them, but so far, no one was asking any questions, and Faith was grateful that her aunt had come through for them in their time of need. The same couldn't be said of her own mother. Even now, Faith could feel Farrow's disapproving gaze boring into her back like a knife. Ultimately, Farrow had relented and allowed them to double up on the funeral services because, in her mother's words, *it wasn't Lynne's fault that her daughter was a traitorous bitch*. So here they were, donned in black from head to toe, staring down at two giant holes in the earth that signified the end of two beautiful lives. Phoebe laid her head on her shoulder, and the comforting gesture broke her heart all over again. She would always be here for Phoebe, but she knew the teen would never be the same after the loss of her twin.

It had only been a few days since the doppelgänger attack, and in that short amount of time, Farrow had officially gone off the reservation, vowing to hunt Sarin to the ends of the Earth. Faith was just as guilty as Sarin, if not more so, for bringing the doppelgänger into existence, but Farrow refused to see the truth. Something about Sarin had always rubbed Farrow the wrong way, and all the hush-hush about the Delvaux witches and Sarin's father had been glaring red flags that Faith had chosen to ignore. That ignorance stopped today. She'd been naive, but now, her eyes were open. The night before the funeral had been bizarre. Farrow had disappeared into the woods behind their home only to return the following day, covered in fifth and reeking of magical residue. Faith had no idea what her mother was up to inside those woods, but after they put Selene and Lynne to rest, she had every intention of finding out. Even now, on this horrible day filled with goodbyes, her mother's eyes seemed vacant and empty. This new blankness was a drastic pivot for someone who'd been raging and wrathful just days before.

As the first shovel of dirt was tossed on the shiny oak box that held Selene's body, the wind picked up, tossing over a few chairs and blowing the flowers off the top of her casket. Fallon motioned for them to pause as she scrambled to put everything back in place. Strange atmospheric anomalies like that had been happening at random since Selene's death, and Faith wondered if Phoebe was finally manifesting her latent powers. Most witches came into their powers around puberty, but by age seventeen, neither of the twins had manifested any significant hints of magic. Sarin suspected foul play, but once again, Faith had chosen not to question her family. Growing up, Farrow and Fallon had refused to let any of them practice magic, claiming it was for their protection, but that irresponsible train of thought was one of the many reasons they were standing here today. Witches without proper training made mistakes, big life-altering mistakes that ended in blood and death. The wind howled, and when Faith looked over at Phoebe, the girl seemed oblivious to the fact that she might be the cause of it. Shrouded in a bubble of grief and pain, her young cousin was a ticking time bomb of magic waiting to explode. Fallon motioned for Phoebe to come to her, and as Faith watched them embrace, the rain came.

Selene's loss was a tragedy, and as she watched Fallon and Phoebe mourn together, she swore she heard a soft voice whisper: *the winds of suffering dance over a sea of rage.* And damn if those words didn't perfectly describe her aunt and cousin in that moment. They were air and water locked together in anguish. She wondered what power Selene might have manifested had her life not been taken so early. Farrow had dominion over earth magic, while Fallon could manipulate water. If Phoebe was manifesting air magic, then their family's power was a representation of four of the five elements. Maybe Selene would have manifested the missing spirit element to round out all five because nothing felt in balance without her. Standing in the pouring rain, she felt numb as she said goodbye to her cousin. Throwing a single white rose on top of the casket, Faith watched with disdain as the mud turned the pristine petal a dirty shade of brown.

Sighing, she left the cemetery with a heavy heart and a renewed desire to try and restore what was left of her family, starting with her mother.

39

CHAPTER 6

Sarin woke up with a sore neck and an ache inside her chest that had nothing to do with her awkward sleeping position on the edge of the sofa. Stretching, she was surprised and a little alarmed to find herself alone in the cabin's living room. Haven's bedroom door was closed, but the shuffling sounds coming from the other side of the door confirmed that she hadn't been abandoned. Taking a deep breath, she tried to relax, knowing that Haven was only a few feet away. She'd never had a problem being alone before, but now, the very idea of it made her blood run cold. Staring up at the ceiling, she wondered when she'd become this crazy, neurotic person. The loud growl from her stomach shifted her focus away from her ruminating thoughts. The hunger pains were a stark reminder of how long she'd gone without eating. Not wanting to bother Haven, she shuffled into the tiny L-shaped area that barely passed as a kitchen and began fishing around in the compact refrigerator for something to soothe the savage beast in her belly. The fridge was well stocked, but as she sized up the contents, the idea of actually consuming any of it made her stomach turn sour. She was in a battle royal between her body's basic needs and the monster named Anxiety. It was all fun times all around. Checking the cabinets for something less intimidating, she was grateful when she came across a pack of unopened Saltines. Pouring a big glass of water, she leaned back against the counter and took a slow, controlled bite of one of the crackers. When the first one stayed down, she felt safe enough to try another.

The urge to call Faith was intense, but she hesitated to use her cell phone. Haven claimed the cloaking spell was working, but her cousin had also mentioned that cell phones could be tracked using non-magical means. The cabin had an old-school landline mounted on the kitchen wall that beckoned her. It was a glossy red beacon of hope. Was it a violation to use it without asking Haven first? She wasn't sure, but she didn't want to risk the chance of her cousin saying no. This was too important. Scrambling across the kitchen like the floor was made of lava, she ripped the phone off its receiver with a shaky hand. She hadn't used a push phone in forever, but luckily, she knew Faith's number by heart. Pressing in the numbers one by one, it took all her inner strength not to vomit as she waited for her best friend to answer or ignore the unknown number. When the call went to voice mail, Sarin set the phone back in its holder and froze as a horrible thought crossed her mind. What if she never got to talk to Faith again? Faith had given her the final push to leave town with Haven, with promises to take care of her mother. But what if that moment had really been goodbye? What if Farrow had interfered and Faith hadn't been able to keep her promise? Bile rose in her throat, and when she leaned over the sink, the crackers and stomach acid finally flew free. It wasn't her finest moment. Soft hands pulled her hair away from her face as she continued to dry heave. Thankful for the small act of kindness, she turned on the faucet and rinsed her mouth before facing her cousin.

"Do you want to talk about it?" Haven asked gently.

Her cousin wore a bright green sweater that complimented her vivid green eyes.

Leaning back against the counter, she used a wet paper towel to wipe her face. "I used the landline to call Faith, but she didn't pick up. I hope you're not mad."

Haven's gaze was assessing but kind. "Answers usually come when they're meant to, even though the waiting sucks. And no, I'm not mad, but next time, ask me first. The cloaking spell should stop any magical attempts at finding us, and that type of phone doesn't have GPS, but the coven could still try and track the number to this address."

Sarin's shoulders slumped in defeat. "Shit! This really sucks!"

"Are anxiety attacks a new thing?" Haven asked as she pulled out a large skillet from underneath the sink.

Instead of installing new cabinet doors on the bottom shelves, the owner had simply hung a dated flower-patterned fabric in front of it and called it a day.

"I've had them my entire life. But they've been getting worse since I started practicing magic. Anything that feels out of my control is a trigger."

"Sounds about right," Haven admitted. "I used to have them all the time as a kid. Seems like red hair isn't the only trait we have in common. I don't know about you, but keeping busy helps me tamp down my anxious thoughts when they get really bad, and I can sense all that pent-up nervousness churning around inside of you. Are you up for a little supervised spell-casting lesson later today?"

"I'm not sure if there's anything that can tamp down the shitstorm of nerves I have raging inside of me, but I need to learn, and it's not like I have time to sign up for a therapy session right now."

Haven walked over to the small refrigerator and pulled out a carton of eggs. "First, I'm going to cook you a proper breakfast since you left most of your crackers in the sink. Then, we'll head out to a clearing in the woods. I could really use your help getting a magical read on something I found out there."

Sarin was hesitant to leave the safety of the cabin. "I thought we needed to stay put. What if Farrow finds us out there?"

Haven cracked the eggs into a small bowl before whisking them. "I've been thinking about that a lot this morning. I want to help you, Sarin, I really do, but I came here for reasons of my own, and I can't stay hidden inside this cabin indefinitely. If you'll let me, I'm going to cast the same cloaking spell on you that I cast on the cabin. I was so worried about getting you away from the coven yesterday that I didn't stop to think about the bigger picture. Do you have a personal item you feel comfortable wearing all the time? Something small that I can imbue with the spell?"

She touched the bracelet on her right wrist. It was a thin gold chain that she hardly ever took off. Unclasping the delicate piece of metal, she handed it over to Haven, who traded her for a plate of steaming hot eggs. As she choked down the food, she hoped Haven's theory about staying busy worked because if it didn't, she felt like she might explode from all the pressure inside her chest.

•••

Two hours and one spelled bracelet later, Sarin found herself pacing around the desolate clearing like a kid in a candy store. "Can't you feel it?"

"I feel my patience slipping," Haven scoffed.

She noted the annoyance in her cousin's voice but didn't comment on it. Maybe she was frustrated that a novice Witch was more in tune with the magic in this land than she was. Or maybe she was PMSing.

"Seriously, it feels like the ground is alive. You asked me to come here to get my take on the clearing, so here it is. Try to be open to the possibility that this place isn't a puzzle only you were meant to solve."

"I felt what you're describing the first time I came here, but I haven't gotten a blip of it since. Give me your hand."

She didn't hesitate, and when they joined hands, she flinched as a freight train of power washed over her.

Gasping, Haven gripped her hand harder. "It's still here, but it's like I'm blocked from it. How can that be?"

"Is there a spell in your book that can remove this kind of barrier?" Sarin asked through clenched teeth. The power rushing through her body was unrelenting.

"I don't know, but now that I can feel it again, it's too much. Let go of my hand!" Haven pleaded.

Sarin tried and failed to pull her hand back from Haven's, and when a fresh wave of panic washed over her, she stared into Haven's equally freaked-out eyes as the forest scene around them melted away and was replaced by something else, something darker. The new landscape was a total contrast to the thriving forest they'd just been standing in. This place was cold and dark and pulsed with an otherworldly emptiness.

"Haven." A distorted voice called out through the darkness.

"Mom?" Haven called back.

A shadow approached from the left.

"How did you find me? You weren't supposed to find me."

No, not a shadow, she realized; it was a person cloaked in billowing gray robes.

The question hadn't been directed at Sarin, but through this strange connection with Haven, it felt like it had. Then, Sarin's brain was overrun with memories. Flashes of Haven's mother running through the dark forest, feet bleeding as she ran for her life. Images of black wings beating through the trees as a nightmarish monster gave chase—scenes of fire, raging and unforgiving, mixed with pleas of those who begged for mercy. A tear rolled down her cheek as realization dawned. The fire she saw, the voices she heard, that was how her father had been killed. These memory blips were a small look into the past when Haven's mother had set her coven ablaze.

"I had to do it," Haven's mother whispered as if responding to Sarin's thoughts. *"I had to be free."*

Haven hadn't told her any of this, but now, under the thrall of whatever strange magic occupied this clearing, Sarin was getting a glimpse of

Haven's family history. Farrow had explained some of this story to her before, but seeing through this insane virtual reality-like experience, made it all too fucking real.

"This place is evil. You girls need to leave and never look back. I was trying to keep it away from you, Haven, but you came back. Don't come back again!"

Before she could ask Haven's mother what she meant, the empty world around them blurred into a kaleidoscope of blues and greens before returning them to the clearing in the forest. Letting go of Haven's hand, she looked up to find her cousin staring back at her through haunted eyes. Haven was visibly shaking and a little pale.

"Tell me what you saw, and please don't sugarcoat it?" Haven asked as she wrapped her arms around herself.

"It was like watching a movie, except I felt everything you felt. I saw everything you saw. Oh god, Haven, you're poor Mother. I'm so sorry!"

Haven let out an audible sigh. "I was going to tell you, but I didn't think you were ready. Not after everything you just went through. And Sarin, that's only a small part of her story. The rest is much worse. Mine is much worse."

Sarin felt completely off-kilter as she paced around the clearing in confusion. They'd been here, then somewhere else, and then back again, all in a matter of seconds, and she was having a hard time processing reality right now.

"I'm ready to listen whenever you want to talk, but for now, can you please tell me where the hell we just went?"

"That's a really good question!" Haven exclaimed. "I don't know if that was a real place or if I just took you with me into a vision, but this proves my mother might still be alive out there, somewhere."

Sarin had a million questions, but as the gravity of Haven's words sank in, she kept her mouth shut. Right now, Haven needed her support and not a Q&A session. She wasn't sure if Haven's mother was dead or alive, but she knew what mother loss felt like, and if she could spare Haven the pain of going through that kind of grief, she'd do anything to try to help her.

CHAPTER 7

Haven was quiet and withdrawn on the walk back from the clearing, and when they finally made it back to the cabin, she shut herself inside her bedroom for some alone time. Sarin understood. The memories they'd shared had been disturbing, and they weren't even hers. Exhausted and still reeling from the ordeal, Sarin sprawled out on the couch and quickly fell into a listless sleep. The dream was the same as the night before. It was the one where she and her mother were sharing breakfast. They were happy and laughing until her mother grabbed a butcher knife from the counter and tried to stab her with it. Then, two things occurred simultaneously: Sarin remembered that her mother was dead, and the facade of her mother's face washed away to reveal the horrifying visage of the doppelgänger. The monster laughed and taunted her for believing the charade before dragging her mother's lifeless body from the pantry to parade it around in front of her.

That's when Sarin woke up, terrified and crying. Pulling the blanket up to her chin for comfort, she sent a silent promise to her mother that once she mastered her powers, she would hunt down the abomination that murdered her and send it back to Hell. The cabin's landline let out a loud shrill that startled her so badly that she fell off the couch. The high-pitched ring was like a glimmer of hope, but after picking herself off the floor, Sarin paused before rushing to answer it. What if it wasn't Faith?

Haven's voice called out from inside the bedroom, "Answer it, Sarin. It's important. We will deal with the consequences as they come."

The nudge was all she needed.

Grappling with the hard piece of plastic, Sarin cursed when she got tangled up in the cord. Pulling the stupid thing off its receiver, she asked, "Faith?"

"Sarin? Is it really you?" her best friend asked from the other end of the line.

Faith's voice washed over her like a warm blanket.

"Yes! I didn't want to use my cell phone, just in case." Pausing, she tried to calm the shakiness in her voice. "How are you?"

"Not good. My mom's officially gone off the deep end, and she won't talk to any of us. I've been trying to keep an eye on her, but Sarin, I'm scared she might be close to finding you. After Selene, I thought she just wanted revenge, but I don't know how I didn't see this obsession with you before. There's always been something about your family that scares her, and I think this goes way beyond Selene's death."

She was trying to pay attention to everything Faith was saying, but she couldn't focus—not until she knew the truth. "Faith, please just tell me what happened with my mom."

"I kept my promise!" Faith declared in a somber tone. "We had her funeral the same day we laid Selene to rest. I'm sorry you couldn't be there."

She never should have doubted her. "Thank you. I'll find a way to pay you back."

"I'm so sorry, Sarin. It shouldn't be this way. Once this all blows over, I'll take you to the cemetery myself, and you can give her a proper goodbye."

The situation wasn't ideal, but at least her mother's body wasn't rotting in their house. "What happened after I left? Are the police doing an investigation?"

"Not yet. Fallon worked her magic on the cops who came by to question us, but I have no idea how long her spells will last. She's not in her right mind at the moment."

Sarin felt for Fallon. Losing her mother felt suffocating at times, but she couldn't begin to fathom the pain of losing a child.

Lowering her voice, Faith added, "You need to lay low. My Mom's been leaving every night and cloaking herself so we can't follow her. She's up to something, Sarin, and until I figure out what it is, you need to stay hidden."

"What exactly do you think I'm doing out here, having a fun-filled camping trip?"

Faith snorted, and the sound warmed Sarin's heart.

"I just don't want anything bad to happen to you. Shit, I have to go, but now that I know this is your number, I'll stay in touch. And Sarin, I love you!"

"I love you too," Sarin replied as her emotions took over.

The line disconnected, and when she looked up, she found Haven staring at her from the other side of the room. "Did you get what you needed?"

Nodding, she placed the phone back in its holder and froze. So many feelings were coming at her all at once. She felt relief that her mother had been properly laid to rest, extreme guilt over the fact she hadn't been there to do it herself, anger over how it had all shaken out, and the bottomless well of grief. There was so much grief. Sprinkle in the worries over being hunted by Farrow and the implications of a possible police investigation, and it was too much.

"Take a breath, Sarin," Haven urged in a calming voice.

It was too late for that. The emotions swelled and grew until they had nowhere to go, and right when Sarin felt like she might explode from the weight of it all, a bright white light erupted from her body in a massive explosion of magic-fueled energy. She heard a loud crash followed by the sounds of Haven cursing, but she didn't care. The relief of letting it all go was too gratifying. Then she was on the floor, and Haven was looming over her, frantically waving her hands in the air. Her cousin's mouth was moving, but she couldn't hear the words over the loud roaring in her ears. Then Haven's worried face disappeared completely as Sarin's world faded to black.

CHAPTER 8

Faith left the cemetery alone. Her mother had disappeared as soon as the rains had come in, and now, the infuriating woman wasn't answering her cell phone. Faith had scoured the grounds of the funeral home for thirty minutes looking for her before finally deciding to leave. She had the car keys, so if her mother wanted to pull a stunt like this on today of all days, then the crazy bitch could figure out her own way home. Fallon and Phoebe had chosen to stay behind, and she understood why. They wanted more time with Selene, even if it was just to say their final goodbyes.

On the drive through downtown Huntsville, she was surprised to find the streets mostly empty. This area of town was usually hopping on the weekends, but maybe there was a big event going on elsewhere. Truth be told, she'd been too wrapped up in her family drama and funeral planning to notice much else. She'd also been picking up shifts at Mills over on Main Street to try and pay her mother back for the cost of Lynne's funeral. Bartending was easy money, but the added hours took time away from school, and she was falling behind in her Nursing Program. Given the death in the family, her school had been flexible with her, but the pile of makeup work was pushing her graduation date farther and farther away. As soon as the thought crossed her mind, she wanted to kick herself for being so selfish. Sarin was in the same program, but her friend didn't have the luxury of waltzing in and talking to the administration about the death of her mother. Becoming a nurse meant everything to Sarin, but Faith knew the school was going to kick her out if she didn't return soon.

A rogue squirrel came out of nowhere, and she had to slam on the brakes to avoid hitting it. The tiny little fur ball didn't seem the least bit concerned about the hulking piece of machinery in front of it as it meandered in the road, looking for who knew what. Beeping the horn to try and get its attention, she gasped when the tiny creature turned its scruffy head in her direction. Its large set of violet-colored eyes that stared back at her were unnerving. She'd never seen a squirrel with eyes that color, and curiosity got the best of her as her brain tried to make sense of the strange sight. Putting the car in park, she got out to get a closer look. As she approached the tiny creature, it finally got with the stranger danger program and darted toward the river with fur that seemed to shimmer in the warm afternoon sun. But that couldn't be right. Feeling a bit dazed, she climbed back into her car and drove the rest of the way home.

Pulling into the driveway, she noticed her dad was home. He'd skipped the funeral - no doubt at her mother's request, and had gone to work instead. Faith wasn't sure what her father thought about her mother's recent behavior, but historically speaking, he rarely had an opinion that contradicted Farrow's. Before the shit with Sarin had gone down, she'd always assumed her dad was just an easy-going kind of guy who preferred to let her mother run the ship. Now, she wondered if more magic and lies were the real reason for his calm demeanor. There was no time like the present to try to pry information out of him, especially since her mother was MIA. She found him mulling around the kitchen, making a sandwich. How he could eat on a day like this was beyond her.

Trying to act all causal, Faith opened the fridge and pulled out a lemon-flavored La Croix. She wasn't thirsty, but it gave her an excuse to be in the kitchen. "Hey, Dad."

"How are you holding up?" he asked before taking a big bite of what appeared to be a ham and Swiss.

"Not well. You?"

He finished chewing before answering. "I'll manage. I'm more concerned about you and your mother."

This was her opening. "Speaking of Mom, do you know where she is?"

His nonchalant shrug spoke volumes. "Your mother said she needed some time alone. When she's ready to talk, she will. You know how she is."

"Yeah, I get that, but she disappeared from the funeral today, and I think it's weird that she's been leaving at night and not coming back until morning. Don't you?"

His brow wrinkled like he was trying really hard to remember something before the mask of calm slid back into place. "I trust your mother irrevocably."

She couldn't believe he was in so much denial about her mother's behavior. "But what reason did she give you for why she's leaving at night? I mean, you're not the least bit curious. What if she's cheating on you?"

Her dad needed to wake up. Right now, he was the only sane parent she had left.

"Your mother and I have been married for a long time, and I've learned not to question her until she's ready. I trust that she has our best interest in mind, and I'm letting her live her life."

"That's not enough for me!" she yelled, slamming her drink on the counter.

Her dad shrugged again, and for the first time in her life, she felt like slapping him. He was either spelled or just really fucking stupid.

"Then you should talk to her, honey. I know the two of you can work it out."

With nothing left to say, her dad took his plate into the living room and left her there to fume. Thankfully, Fallon and Phoebe chose that moment to walk through the front door. They didn't live here, but they'd been staying over since Selene's passing. Fallon and her husband had separated a while back, and her aunt didn't want to be alone in her house. Speaking of Fallon, her aunt was unusually quiet as she poured herself a cup of coffee and sat down at the breakfast nook.

Phoebe took one look at her and knew something was up. "Why do you look all flustered and sweaty? BT dubs, it's not a good look for you."

Now wasn't the time to burden Phoebe with anything heavy, so she chose to tell her about the strange squirrel rather than discuss her hypothesis about her dad being a walking, talking puppet.

"Are you sure you didn't hit your head on something? You know how clumsy you are," Phoebe teased.

"It was real! I'm not insane!"

Phoebe tapped her forefinger on her chin. "You know what. I believe you. I mean, we're clearly living in an alternate reality where my sister is dead, so mutant squirrels running rampant around town seems very on point."

Phoebe always used humor to deflect her true feelings.

"Can we have a movie marathon tonight? Please?" Phoebe begged with emphasis.

"Are you sure you're feeling up to that, Pheebs?"

"I'm compartmentalizing and can't deal with my feelings, so absolutely."

Her heart constricted under the weight of her words." I'm in, but I had to pick up a shift at Mills tonight, so I won't be home until ten-ish. Is that too late?"

Phoebe's eyes lit up with a mischievous glint. "I'll just force my mom to watch whatever I want until it's your turn."

Faith was elated her cousin had a plan—any plan—other than crying herself to sleep. "Great. That will give you plenty of time to pick out the perfect one for us."

"Oh, I already know which one. Cabin in the Woods. Mom's skittish and won't watch any scary stuff with me, so I'm saving that one for you."

"Pheebs, we've watched that movie like a hundred times. Do you really think horror is the right genre to end the day on?"

"I think I like that movie, and since it's my choice, you can suck it," Phoebe so eloquently declared as she walked out of the kitchen.

Sometimes, she forgot her cousin was only seventeen and a ball of raging hormones.

"Fine, fine!" she conceded. "Auntie, why are you being so quiet and stalkerish over there?"

Her aunt's lip quirked up in a small smile, and Faith was happy to see something other than sorrow plastered on her beautiful face. "I'm not stalking, just observing."

"You saw her use her powers today, right?" She needed to be sure she wasn't imagining things.

"I did, but she didn't seem to notice, and that's okay with me for now. New powers can be volatile even with a steady mind, and Phoebe's is anything but. I believe you about the squirrel, by the way. Yesterday, when we were at the funeral home, making the final arrangements, I saw something strange too. You know that little pond on the right side of the cemetery?"

She did. She'd walked right by it when they'd gone out to the burial site this morning.

"Well, I was standing there watching the fish swim around when this strange ripple undulated through the water. I wouldn't have noticed if I hadn't been staring right at it. It was just a tiny blip, but afterward, all the fish floated to the surface. I put my hands in the water to see if my powers could tell me what was going on, but all I felt was a void of nothingness. It's like the ripple sucked all the life out of the pond."

Leaning back against the counter, Faith crossed her arms over her chest. "Have you ever witnessed anything like that before?"

"No, and normally, I would defer to Farrow about things like this, but she hasn't been around."

"Speaking of the devil. Do you know where she is? Tweedle-dad over in the living room doesn't have a clue."

"Your father cares, but my sister's been casting spells on him for way too long. At this point, I wouldn't be surprised if he has some sort of magical induced dementia."

She was shocked by her aunt's honest admission. "And you just sat back and watched her do it? What does that say about you?"

Fallon flinched like Faith had physically slapped her. "There are consequences to going against your mother. I've stayed silent for years, but now, I feel like everything's gone too far."

The words were pretty, but Faith needed action. "So, what exactly do you plan to do about it?"

Her aunt pegged her with an intense stare. "Not me, Faith. *We*. What are *we* going to do about it? I can't take my sister on alone, and Phoebe isn't ready for that fight. Are you willing to do whatever it takes to stop your mother from hurting Sarin?"

She loved her mother, but the woman had officially gone AWAL. "Yes, I am!"

"Then we need to figure out what she's been doing in the woods and find a way to cut her off from her magic. If she can't access her powers, she's less of a threat."

Faith cringed when she realized what time it was. "Shit. I have to go to work, but we need to make a plan when I get back. Do you know any spells that can help us neutralize her?"

Fallon's eyes turned grim. "We only have one family grimoire, and it's the one she keeps locked in her room."

"This situation just keeps getting more and more complicated," Faith huffed. "The last time I stole her book to try to help Sarin, I think I just got lucky. I'm sure she has better security measures in place now."

"I'm sorry this is happening, Faith. I know your mother loves you, but something's wrong with her. I can feel it. She's always been self-righteous and driven, but this obsession with Sarin and all the excessive lying, especially to me, isn't like her."

Faith felt the tears coming and she looked at the ceiling to try and hold them back. She needed to get ready for work and didn't have time for an emotional breakdown right now.

"I'm sorry, too. I'll never be able to forgive myself for my part in Selene's death, and I refuse to have anyone else's blood on my hands. I love my mom, but I won't let her hurt Sarin."

Fallon walked over and pulled Faith in for a tight hug. "I love you, Faith, and it's not your fault. We're a family, and we protect what's ours, even from each other when necessary. I've seen the wonder and destruction magic can bring, and your mother's mind is clouded. It's time for us to bring her back to the light."

Faith wasn't so sure there was any light to bring her mother back to. Her mother's essence had always felt dark to her, and that was long before she'd gone off the magical reservation. Staring into her aunt's hope-filled eyes, she didn't have the heart to tell her how she truly felt. So, for now, she kept her mouth shut and prayed Fallon knew her twin sister's soul better than she did.

CHAPTER 9

The bar pulsed with an otherworldly energy. The patrons didn't realize what was causing their distress, but the doppelgänger could feel the raw magic lingering in the air. Working behind the bar, it surveyed its prey. It was desperate to feed, to destroy, but taking a human life meant it had to assume that person's form, and it needed to keep its current visage for its revenge plan to work. Staring at its reflection in the ornate mirror behind the bar, it studied its borrowed face. Finding the young boy sitting alone by the back of the bar after the red-haired witch had attempted to banish it had been pure luck. Then, it had been a simple matter of ending his life and tossing his worthless corpse into the muddy waters of the Muskoka River. The killing had been easy, but keeping up the ruse was trying, especially now that the young witch named Faith was picking up shifts at the bar. The witch knew Alex well, and even with access to the boy's memories, it was finding it hard to keep up the facade. The stupid blonde asked too many questions.

It had chosen Alex's form because it provided access and proximity to its prey. It needed to understand human emotions, relationships, and the peculiarities of their existence in order to kill Sarin Delvaux. After murdering Alex, who just happened to be Sarin's ex-boyfriend, it had taken over his life and job at the bar in the hopes that Sarin would return. But as the nights passed, there had been no sign of the witch, and it was growing impatient. The very thought of Sarin made its body pulse with violent bloodlust.

Faith was also hush-hush about Sarin's whereabouts, claiming the girl was home with the flu. Whatever that was. But innocent little Faith didn't realize she involuntarily tucked her hair behind her ears whenever she lied. It was an obvious tell. Humans were pathetic and predictable that way, and it was baffling they couldn't discern these kinds of behaviors for themselves. They were nothing but a disgusting plague on this Earth.

As the bar buzzed with laughter and obnoxious chatter, it yearned to silence it all. Gripping the pint glass in its hand, it surveyed the rowdy crowd with disdain. All these sweaty humans were packed together shoulder to shoulder, drinking down poison to try to temporally forget the pain of their meaningless lives. If they wanted an out, it would be more than happy to provide them with a grotesque and bloody death. It envisioned all the ways it could end them, but deep down, it knew the thrill of killing any of these pathetic meat suits would only be fleeting. It wanted Sarin, and only her demise would satiate its rage. In truth, it found this human existence to be boring and monotonous. Alex's memories provided the blueprint it needed to survive in this world, but even those felt lackluster. How these humans survived without the thrill of the hunt was beyond its understanding. They were nothing but walking, talking cattle, and once it killed Sarin and took her powers, it would subjugate them all before indulging in every delight this existence had to offer.

Faith swept in through the employee entrance, surrounded by her usual air of self-righteousness, and it took all its composure not to reach over and peel the platinum-dyed scalp off her head. In its true form, it had scars covering both of its arms from where Faith had burned it using her fire magic. Being this close to her was dangerous, especially when it wanted nothing more than to watch her bleed out. It had fantasies about torturing her and using her to draw Sarin out, but in this human form, it didn't have any powers, and going up against a witch, even a fledgling one like Faith, was a bad idea. The witch served a purpose, just like its visage. So, instead of bashing in her skull, it swallowed down its rage and waved at the bitch before adding in a little wink for good measure. The second move was a trademark of Alex's.

As the night ticked on and the drinks continued to flow, the conversations in the bar turned from light-hearted nonsense to more serious topics. There was talk of strange electrical outages all over the city, whispers about animals becoming violent, and stories of unnerving sounds coming from the woods. The residents were scared, and no one could make sense of what was happening. Since it had been born from magic, it was connected to it, and it knew without question that something very ancient was lurking deep inside the woods the humans spoke of. Wiping the stale beer off the counter, it shuddered in ecstasy as a wave of magic ripped through the bar. Whatever was coming for this town had the power to destroy everything in its wake, and it had no intention of sticking around to join the lemmings in their annihilation. If Sarin didn't reappear on her own, soon, it would have no choice but to move on to more colorful revenge tactics, starting with the blonde witch at the end of the bar.

CHAPTER 10

Haven sat in the wrecked living room, gently wiping her cousin's face with a cold compress. Sarin's breathing was even, but the girl had been out cold for hours. She tried everything to try and wake her; talking, physical prodding, even splashing cold water on her face, but nothing worked, and when Sarin's fever spiked, she panicked. Pulling out her mother's grimoire, she searched for a spell to try to rouse her, but thankfully, logic caught up to her fear-filled mind, and she stopped herself. Sarin's body had just expelled a shit ton of pent-up mystical energy and adding any magic back in didn't seem like a good idea right now, no matter how worried she was. The explosion of light that had burst from Sarin's body had been like a mini energy bomb, knocking her on her ass and decimating the living room in its path of destruction. The terrified look on

Sarin's face told Haven she'd had no warning or control over it, and that didn't bode well for either of them. Chairs had been overturned, and shards of glass from the broken coffee table were scattered all over the room. After the exorcist-like expulsion, Sarin had collapsed, and now, here they were. If she couldn't teach her cousin to control her powers, and soon, the girl was liable to do this again, and if she passed out in the face of the enemy, it was game over. Dipping the washcloth in a small bowl of water, she dappled more of the cold liquid across Sarin's forehead. Sarin's eyes darted around back and forth behind her closed lids, and she let out a soft, pain-filled moan. The sound was progress, but her fever still raged. Haven covered her cousin with a warm blanket before shuffling her way around the broken furniture and debris to lie on the couch. She was exhausted, and there wasn't much more she could do for Sarin until she woke up. If that didn't happen soon, she'd be forced to use her magic to intervene. Consequences be damned.

As she fell into a listless sleep, Lucifer visited her once again. The scenery was different this time, but his overbearing presence remained the same. He looked imposing and smug as he lounged back on a cream-colored leather sofa in the middle of what appeared to be a large living space. The floors were made of polished black marble that reflected the warm glow of firelight emanating from the large fireplace in the corner, and somehow, despite its grand size, the room felt cozy and intimate.

"Where are we?" she asked in awe of the space.

"This is my private chamber, and I don't allow many to come here. You should feel privileged."

Her stomach dropped. Lucifer didn't live on Earth, so if they were in his private space, this was bad. Very, very bad. "You mean we're in Hell?"

"If I said yes, would you leave? Honestly, you don't seem like the skittish type."

His flirty tone gave her the sinking feeling that this was all part of some sadistic game. Maybe his new tactic was an attempt at seduction? She hated how much that thought made her heart race. She didn't even like him, so why was her body reacting this way?

"Why do you keep showing up in my dreams? Don't you have better things to do? Like, oh, I don't know, run Hell? We're not friends, so if you want something from me, spit it out so I can get back to my life."

Taking a sip of the dark red liquid swirling around in his glass, he stared at her with an assessing look. "What if all I want is to get to know you better?"

She couldn't stifle the laugh. This couldn't be real. They barely knew each other, and his help with the whole apocalypse situation had been for his benefit only. "Is this some weird dream date? Because if I'm being honest, you seem less of a *let's talk* and more of a *let's get naked and down to the business* type of guy."

The wicked glint in his eyes told her just how spot-on she was in her assessment. Playing into his bullshit, she strode toward him, stopping just between his knees.

Lucifer seemed surprised by the move, but she made her intentions clear when she leaned in. "I don't have time for cryptic little games. So, either tell me what you want from me or leave me the fuck alone!"

To her utter shock, Lucifer leaned forward and claimed her lips with a non-human speed that made her head spin. Her first instinct was to pull away, but when his lips brushed over hers for a second time, her traitorous body gave in and kissed him back. He slowly slid his hands up the backs of her thighs, giving her plenty of time to stop him before he pulled her into his lap. Her body felt like a live wire on top of his, and she arched into him before deepening the kiss. Gripping her by the waist, he held her in place as he moved his mouth from her lips to the column of her neck. As he explored her body with his mouth, she caught sight of their reflection in the mirror behind the couch, and what she saw in the etched glass made her blood run cold. She looked the same, but Lucifer was depicted in his true form. He had long ebony horns extending out from both sides of his head, and his massive wings were see-through and bat-like, with bony ridges that protruded from both ends. His smooth, tanned skin had taken on an ashy-like sheen, and long black talons replaced the soft hands that still gripped her by the waist. Gasping in shock, she scrambled off his lap.

The glamoured version of Lucifer sitting before her still looked very sexy and slightly disheveled. "You knew who I truly was long before you let me touch you, so why does seeing it now scare you so?"

She didn't have a good answer for him. He was right, but something about this dreamscape had temporarily made her feel safe with him. A falsehood she would remember from now on.

"You are safe with me," he replied, reading her thoughts.

Disgusted with herself for letting him touch her in the first place, she spat. "You're a monster!"

Leaning back against the sofa, a cruel smile crept over his face. "That's rich coming from you. What do you think humans would do to you if they found out what you truly are? Worship at your feet? I think fire and death are more likely, considering the history of your kind. I didn't have a choice about my punishment or what I became because of it, but I wasn't always what you see before you. I've had to accept my fate and all the horrors of this place, but now that God has disappeared, maybe my fate can change."

Ding, ding, ding, she thought, and there it was. "That's the real reason I'm here. You want a way out, just like God did, and you plan on using me to try to accomplish it."

Standing, Lucifer strode toward her until they were nose to nose. "That's the thing, my little witch. I had no intention of leaving Hell until I set my eyes on you. Now, all bets are off."

Haven woke up with a jolt. Her head felt foggy, and there was a strange buzzing sound nearby. Sitting up, she gasped as the scene around her came into stark focus. The living room was swarming with locusts. A large horde of them covered the opposite end of the couch, and they were scurrying straight for her. Panic threatened to paralyze her if she didn't move now. Jumping off the couch, she swatted at the ones flying in the air as she ran toward the front door. Reaching for the handle, a feeling of dread washed over her when the knob refused to budge. Tuning into her magic, she cast the same banishing spell she'd used on the doppelgänger, but nothing happened. It was too late. The bugs covered her from head to toe in a sea of spindly limbs, and when she tried to scream, the locusts silenced the sound as they raced inside her mouth.

•••

Gagging, she rolled over on the couch to catch her breath. Patting her body down, she sighed in relief when she realized the bugs were gone. The locusts had been just another dream. Or had they? Both of the dreams felt equally authentic, but what did the locusts mean? Were they some kind of twisted parting gift sent by Lucifer or a sign of something ominous on the horizon? Nothing was ever simple anymore. If Lucifer wanted to be free of Hell, she wasn't sure she could help him. Or if she should. Everything in the universe came with a cost, and the brand on her palm was a haunting reminder that even with the best intentions, shit could go sideways. Lucifer had helped her stop the apocalypse by fueling a spell to set God free from Heaven. During the biblical Fall, Lucifer, along with his angelic brother Samuel, had been cast out of Heaven for going against God's wishes. Samuel had been tasked with ruling over purgatory and been gifted with a one-year reprieve, while Lucifer had been sent to Hell with no chance of respite. But in the midst of His wrath, God forgot about one significant little fact: whatever was done to one realm was mirrored in all three. So, by locking the fallen angels in their respective realms, God had inadvertently locked himself inside Heaven. To give God the out he wanted without causing the end of the world, Samuel had agreed to transfer his reprieve to Heaven, and Lucifer had been the catalyst they needed to get the job done. Their plan had been a success, but now, if Lucifer was telling the truth, he wanted the same thing. She had no interest in helping another celestial being, even if this one was tall, dark, and infuriatingly handsome. The migraine hit her out of nowhere, and she figured she had two choices. She could sit here and mull over Lucifer's potential plans for her, or she could use his attraction to her advantage the next time they met. She was pulled from her thoughts when Sarin began to stir.

Rushing to her side, Haven cursed when she stepped on a sharp piece of glass. "Shit!"

Sarin's bright green eyes popped open.

Limping the remainder of the way, Haven sank down on the floor beside her. "Sorry, I didn't mean to startle you."

Sarin looked confused as she took in their surroundings. "What happened?"

Picking up a clean washcloth from the pile, she placed it against her bleeding heel. "You kind of blew up."

"Blew up how?" Sarin asked, still seeming dazed.

"A bunch of pent-up magic literally exploded out of your body in a rush of energy. Then you passed out and have been running a fever for the past few hours."

"Faith laid my mom to rest with Selene," Sarin explained as she wiped the sweat-soaked hair away from her forehead.

"I'm glad," Haven responded with a smile. "How are you feeling now?"

Standing on shaky legs, Sarin leaned on the counter to steady herself. "Tired, but okay. Let me help you clean this up."

"I don't think you're in any shape to do that right now. Why don't you sit, and I'll get you some water."

Sarin didn't argue as Haven guided her over to the couch. "I have no idea how this happened."

"You let your emotions get the best of you, and your magic took over."

"Is blunt and direct the only way you know how to communicate?" Sarin asked with a hint of a smile.

Haven shuffled around the broken furniture, careful to avoid any more broken glass as she made her way to the kitchen. "We don't have time for gentle. What do you think will happen if you pass out in the middle of a fight with the doppelgänger? Or Farrow?"

"I know, I know!" Sarin huffed in frustration.

Haven backed off a little. This wasn't her cousin's fault; they just needed to ensure it didn't happen again. "I'm glad you were able to release some of that pent-up emotion, even if it wasn't intentional, but this just proves how badly I need to train you."

"So, what happens now?"

"First, I'm going to force you to eat a sandwich. Then, you're going to go take a shower because, no offense, I can smell you from over here."

Sarin lifted her T-shirt and grimaced when she got a whiff of herself.

"Told you," Haven joked, even though their situation was anything but comical.

CHAPTER II

Faith got home from the bar a little after ten to find Phoebe and her aunt in the throes of a Legally Blonde marathon. Tiptoeing past them, she beelined it toward her room for a quick change of clothes. One major downside to working at Mills was the constant smell of stale beer that clung to her like a second skin. She was almost to her room when her mother stepped into the hall.

Crossing her arms over her chest, Farrow gave her a thorough once-over with her piercing blue eyes that were always judging. "Why are you still working at that shitty bar? The funeral's over, and the money you gave me from your savings account was enough to cover everything."

Her mother hadn't said more than two words to her for days, and now she wanted to chat. Her arrogance was enraging. "I obviously need more money to recoup the money you forced me to give you. Or maybe I just like being at the bar more than being stuck in this house with you. Oh wait, that's right, you're never even here."

Farrow rolled her eyes. "We're not doing this again."

"Doing what?" she demanded.

"I'm your mother, and where I go is none of your business. Don't forget our roles."

"Like you would let me," she said under her breath.

"Excuse me?" her mother questioned.

"Nothing. It's late, and shouldn't you be leaving?"

Her mother flashed her with a smile that was anything but nice. "Yes, actually, I should."

As her mother walked past her, she had an overwhelming urge to trip her.

Stopping at the end of the hall, her mother paused. "Regardless of what you might think, everything I've done is for the safety of this family. I hope you can understand that one day."

She didn't bother to turn around. She was done with all her mother's bullshit rhetoric, so instead of indulging her with a response, she simply stepped inside her bedroom and shut the door. Her mother had never been the warm and cuddly type, but this new blunted version of her was terrifying. Things between them had been slowly deteriorating since they moved to Huntsville. Her mother had chosen this town because of its proximity to the Algonquin National Forest, and since the move, Farrow had developed an unhealthy obsession with finding a secret object hidden somewhere within the miles of uninhabited woodlands. It was just one more secret to add to the never-ending list. Her mother spent most of her weekends dragging her aunt and her father around the woods on random camping trips, leaving her alone to watch over her twin cousins. The adjustment had been hard at first, but things had changed for the better since she met Sarin at school. Farrow hadn't liked Sarin from the get-go, and as they became closer, her mother had gone to great lengths to put a wedge between them. Now, Farrow was out for blood, and her sights were set on Sarin. Faith understood the need for revenge because she wanted it, too, but her rage was pointed at the monster who'd taken the lives of her loved ones and not her best friend.

Her mother's erratic behavior had been on the rise long before Selene's death, and tonight, she and her aunt had a plan to steal her mother's grimoire to try and find a spell to take away her magic. Their plan looked like this: once her mother left for the night, Fallon would cast a sleeping spell on her father so they had enough time to find the book and search her parents' room for whatever else Farrow might be hiding. Then, they would formulate the rest of the plan based on whatever they found. At eleven PM on the dot, Farrow left the house, draped in a black hooded coat. Faith snuck out of her room at the sound of the front door closing and found Fallon in the kitchen, preparing the magic tea for her father.

Whispering, she asked, "What are we going to do about Phoebe? I'm supposed to be taking your place for the movie marathon."

"She passed out on the couch about an hour ago and is currently dead to the world."

Peaking around the corner, Faith confirmed with her own eyes that Phoebe was, in fact, fast asleep on the sofa. Her dad was still awake, but he looked half dead as he reclined back in his lounge chair, watching the movie credits scroll across the TV screen. Once Fallon finished brewing the tea, she mouthed the words to an incantation spell over the warm brew before marching it over to her father. Keeping a lookout, Faith watched as her dad took the steaming cup from Fallon with a nod and a smile. Fallon had managed to mask the bitter taste of the . herbs with lemon and ginger, and when her dad's dark green eyes glazed over, Fallon gently laid his head back against the recliner. A ping of guilt flickered in her stomach. She didn't like deceiving her dad, but desperate times called for desperate measures. Leaving him softly snoring in his, she followed her aunt down the hallway toward her parents' room, but when she reached for the doorknob, Fallon stopped her.

"Can't you feel it?" Fallon asked, gently holding onto her wrist.

The pulse of magic was subtle. She'd been so eager to go all guns blazing that she hadn't noticed it at all. "Is it spelled? Can you reverse it?"

Rubbing her hands together, Fallon mouthed the words to a spell that sounded a lot like French before she grabbed hold of the knob. An audible sizzle rang out, and Faith gagged as the smell of burnt flesh filled the air. Fallon didn't so much as flinch as a thick cloud of steam rose up around her, and the lock opened with a click.

Faith gaped at the sight of the angry welt on her aunt's hand. "Oh my god! Are you okay?"

"It's nothing one of my creams can't fix," Fallon commented as she shook out her hand.

Fallon could manipulate water, and her trick with the steam had been impressive.

"What kind of spell did she have on it?"

"A simple but effective one. The knob was spelled to burn whoever opened it, so I used my water magic to essentially douse the flame. I'll have to re-cast her spell when we're done and glamour my hand for a few days until this heals."

"Thank you for helping me," Faith said with sincerity. She couldn't begin to imagine how hard this was for her aunt; her mother was her twin sister, after all.

Her aunt flashed her a sad-looking smile before ushering her into the bedroom, and when they stepped inside, she stopped short at the sight of the mess. Farrow prided herself on being organized and tidy, so the state of the room was a shock. Mud-stained clothes were strewn all about, and dirty footprints littered the floor.

"Look at the prints, Faith. The path leads from here to the closet."

Following the proverbial breadcrumbs, Faith switched on the light inside her parent's walk-in closet. "I don't understand. There's nothing here."

Walking past her, Fallon pressed her hands against the wall. "You're only looking with your eyes. Look again, with your magic."

"I don't know how," she admitted. She'd never been trained to use her powers.

"We really did you girls a disservice, didn't we?" Fallon said with a sigh. "I wish I had listened to my gut and trained the twins; then maybe Selene would still be alive."

"You can't blame yourself, auntie. You did what you thought was right at the time."

"It was a mistake I plan to remedy with you and Phoebe as soon as we get a handle on my sister. Look, over there, do you see that line in the wood plank that doesn't match the rest of the tongue and groove pattern in the floor?"

Closing her eyes, Fallon chanted the words to another spell, and when she raised her right hand, the panel on the floor flew up to reveal a hidden compartment underneath. Lying inside the small hidey-hole was an old leather-bound journal.

"Well, shit," Faith declared as she sat down. "That's not the grimoire!"

Pulling out the journal, Fallon closed the wood panel before sitting beside her. "No, but it's something. Better get comfy; we only have until morning to decipher whatever's inside this thing."

CHAPTER 12

Farrow shuffled through the mud and the rain just like she had for the past two nights. She regretted the harsh words she'd spat at her daughter, but she needed to keep her safe until this was all over. Once Sarin was dead, there would be no one left to challenge her, and their family could start over, utilizing all the power they'd been denied until now. Trudging through the thick woods, she closed her eyes and let the drops of rain splatter against her too-warm skin. The cool water offered a temporary reprieve from all the guilt and rage burning inside of her. Everything would be worth it in the end; she truly believed that. Walking farther into the trees, she waited until she was fully engulfed by the night before teleporting herself to the clearing. She hadn't told Fallon about The Void. She hadn't told her sister the truth about a lot of things. Reappearing inside the clearing under the light of the full moon, she waited for the call, just like she had every other night. The undiluted magic near The Void was so powerful it threatened to bring her to her knees.

"Come to me, daughter!" the alluring voice whispered from inside The Void.

It was the same demand, night after night. She wanted this, but the small part of her that still yearned to be a mother had overridden the thrill of the dark invitation until now. Tonight, the call was a frantic command she could no longer deny. Letting the insidious voice wash over her, Farrow let go of everything she was and surrendered herself to The Void. Her soul purred in satisfaction as The Void's velvety dark magic washed over her in waves of pure ecstasy. This was what her ancestors had wanted for her all along.

"Yield all that you are, and I will make you a God!"

"Yes!" she screamed. She would give her very soul to harness the power The Void was offering.

"And so you shall," The Void answered in a menacing voice.

Dropping to her hands and knees, Farrow screamed as its dark power swept over her, washing away everything she was and replacing it with something new. Black tendrils of smoke darted inside every orifice of her being as her body was lifted off the hard-packed earth by a pair of phantom hands. Floating in mid-air, her inhuman transformation began. It was pain. It was death. It was a rebirth.

Her fingers elongated into bony-shaped appendages before sprouting sharp black-tipped claws. Horns sprouted from the sides of her head as her legs doubled in size and strength. Her skin was ripped apart and twisted back together before transforming into a new bark-like texture. Fangs dropped down from her gums, and thick green vines sprouted from her skin before wrapping themselves around her body like a protective armor. Then, her face turned gaunt and doe-like as dark-colored flowers erupted from the vines covering her new skin.

Once the transformation was complete, her body was lowered to the ground by the same invisible hands that had been holding it in place. She was strong and connected to the forest in a way she'd never imagined. The life force of the trees pulsed inside her veins, and she could see the world through the eyes of the animals around her. It was beautiful and overwhelming. This power was hers by birthright, and the humans would pay for what they'd done to her kin, starting with Sarin.

"Not yet. You're my protector now," The Void commanded.

She hissed through her new set of fangs, "I didn't agree to be anyone's protector. I have plans of my own!"

An invisible wave of power knocked her off her feet and propelled her body into the trunk of a nearby tree. Vines shot out of the tree, tying themselves around her ankles and wrists to hold her in place.

"You will do my bidding!" The Void demanded.

The vines wound their way along her legs and arms until they enveloped her completely.

Struggling, she thrashed against her living captors, but it was no use. "You're the ultimate power. Why do you need me?"

"Stop the ones who come for me. Then you will be free."

As her new body became one with the tree, she howled in outrage. She would remain trapped until whatever rested inside The Void chose otherwise.

"What did you do to me? What am I?" she demanded.

The Void whispered a single word in response. "Dryad."

CHAPTER 13

Sitting with her head resting against the wall of her mother's closet, Faith waited for her aunt to say anything about what they'd discovered inside Farrow's secret journal. The woman was eerily calm even though Faith could feel the betrayal radiating off of her in waves.

Fallon's thick brown hair fluttered around her face as she shook her head in denial. "We're twins. How could she have kept this from me for all these years?"

This level of deceit was utterly unfathomable, and Faith didn't have a good answer for her aunt. Her mother had lied to all of them for her entire fucking life. Some things made more sense now, like her instant bond with Sarin and her mother's disdain for the girl from the get-go. It was all there, spelled out on the yellowed pages of an old, worn-down journal.

Fallon's face was flushed, and her eyes were puffy from crying. "Did you know I followed her into the woods one night?"

Faith hadn't known that, but she stayed silent while her aunt explained.

"I didn't know what else to do. I thought I was being stealthy, but Farrow knew I was there the entire time, and when I got too close, she used her magic on me. On me! Her own sister. She unearthed a tree and let it fall right in front of me, and when I looked up in shock, she was staring right at me. Then she teleported into thin air, and we haven't spoken about it since."

Faith didn't know what to say to her aunt. Her mother's actions were unforgivable, and after what she'd just read in the journal, she didn't know who her mother really was anymore—or who she really was, for that matter. "So, what do we do now?"

Fallon looked as lost as she felt. "Thanks to that journal, we know where she's been going, so now, we pick a night and confront her in that clearing."

"Are you sure that's a good idea?" she asked.

"What other choice do we have, Faith?" Waving the journal in the air, her aunt added, "It's not like she's going to come clean about any of this."

"You're right," she said in a defeated voice. "We should put the journal back and get out of here in case she comes home."

"We needed to do this soon. I can't..." her aunt paused as a fresh tear streamed down her face. "I don't think I can wait very long to confront my sister."

The weight of it all was too much for her aunt. She'd just lost a daughter, only to find out that her twin sister had deceived her. Faith wanted to hug her, but she got the feeling her aunt needed some space right now.

"I need to talk to Sarin before we confront her. God, auntie, it all makes sense now. Sarin deserves to know the truth in case something happens to us."

Fallon paused just outside the doorway. She opened her mouth to say something but hesitated.

Faith didn't know what to say either, so she asked the first stupid question that came to mind. "Do you want me to help you recast the spell on the knob?"

Shrugging, Fallon shook her head. "What's the point? My sister doesn't give a shit about us, so I don't care about hiding what we did. Talk to Sarin and Faith and let me know when you're ready. I can't begin to imagine what's going on inside your head right now, and I want to be there for you; I really do. But, right now, I need to be alone."

Placing the journal back into its hidden compartment, she wanted to scream at the injustice of it all. If everything in the journal was true, then her mom had discovered the truth about their family years ago. That knowledge was the real reason they'd moved to Canada and the real reason her mother had spent hundreds of hours scouring the forest. Faith's hands shook as she turned off the closet light and left her parents' bedroom. There was no going back and no way to unlearn what she'd just discovered.

Phoebe came shuffling down the hallway, half asleep on her feet.

As she passed by, Faith tried and failed to fake a smile. "Do you need anything, Pheebs?"

Yawning, Phoebe ran a hand through her messy brown waves. "I'm good. Just heading to bed. The couch sucks!"

"I'm sorry I missed our movie night. I got home late. Rain check?"

"Sure," Phoebe said with a hint of a slur. "Night."

Passing through the living room, she saw that her dad was still fast asleep in his reclining chair. He seemed calm and peaceful, and as she looked at him, some of her anger dissipated. Fallon had come clean about Farrow's magic influence over him, and now, she just felt sorry for the man. He was just another pawn in her mother's deceptive games. Leaving him to dream, she shuffled into the kitchen. Her body felt heavy under the weight of the truth, but there was no way her traitorous mind was going to let her rest. Not unless she took matters into her own magical little hands. She was hesitant to cast by herself, especially after what had gone down with Sarin, but there was still some sleepy-time tea leftover from the batch her aunt had prepared for her dad. Sighing, Faith cursed her mother again for not teaching her how to use magic properly. She was a witch, for goodness' sake, and she shouldn't feel scared over casting one simple sleeping spell. Pouring the last of the now cold tea into a mug, she whispered the words she'd heard her aunt chant earlier that night before downing the bitter-tasting liquid. The tea worked a little too well, and she was stumbling by the time she made it to her bedroom. It was a miracle she'd made it this far, and when her knees hit the end of her bed, she face-planted onto her clean, soft sheets and fell into a blissful, dreamless sleep.

•••

"Faith! Wake-up! Hello?"

God, that sing-song voice was annoying, Faith thought through her sleep-filled haze. She'd just laid down. Who could possibly need anything from her right now?

"Come on, Faith. It's after ten already!"

Rolling onto her back, she cracked open her tired eyes to find Phoebe sitting on the side of her bed. The harsh light streaming in through the blinds cast her cousin's face in shadow, making the girl appear much older than she actually was. Or maybe losing your twin did that to a person.

"I don't have to work until tonight, so why do I need to get up?" she grumbled as she pulled the sheet over her face.

"Because you're the only one here, and I'm bored," Phoebe whined. "Plus, you owe me a movie date, and who says we can only watch scary movies at night?"

She didn't want to get out of bed. She didn't want to deal with life or the reality of what she and her aunt had discovered the night before. Here, under the warmth of her cozy blankets, she was safe. But something Phoebe said roused her suspicion.

Pulling the sheet back down, she asked, "What do you mean no one's here?"

"Exactly what I said. The house is empty, except for you, sleeping beauty."

Faith sat up, brushing her blonde waves out of her face, as a horrible realization dawned on her: Her mother hadn't returned this morning.

"Was your mom in the guest room last night when you went to bed?"

Phoebe didn't seem the least bit concerned. "No, but sometimes she goes back to our house at night to take care of stuff. You know that."

That was true, but Faith didn't think that's where she'd gone this time.

Phoebe hopped off the bed, quickly changing the subject. "I'm starving, and you know I suck at cooking. So, if you're not in the mood for a movie, would you please make me some eggs as a consolation prize?"

Smiling despite the rising feeling of panic in her chest, Faith got out of bed and begrudgingly followed Phoebe into the kitchen. The girl was annoying ninety-nine percent of the time, but she had a kind heart. Turning on the coffee pot, she smiled when she pulled out her favorite coffee mug. It had been a gift from Selene that read: *Big Witch Energy.*

Closing the cabinet, she noticed a yellow sticky note stuck to the microwave: *Went to the store. Be back later.* At least her dad was thoughtful enough to leave a note.

"Did you even bother to call your mom before you stomped into my room, demanding all of my attention?" she asked as she opened the fridge.

Phoebe's lips quirked into a sneaky smile. "No, because you're the only person I want to annoy today."

"Lucky me!" she joked. "And we're out of eggs, so toast is all I have to offer."

"I'm serious, Faith! I need you, okay? Selene was the A-type planner in this family, and without her, I don't know what to do with myself."

She had no epic words of wisdom or comfort to offer her cousin, so she just spoke from the heart. "She was your twin, a literal piece of you, and as much I miss her, I can't begin to understand what that's like for you. All we can do is take it day by day, and some days are going to suck."

Putting the toast on a plate, she poured herself a huge cup of coffee before taking a seat next to her cousin at the bar. Sniffling, Phoebe wiped away her tears, which were replaced by a streak of black smudge. The teen was still in her pajamas and must have forgotten to take her makeup off before bed.

"So, can I shadow you today?" Phoebe asked as she took a bite of toast.

Faith wanted to be there for her cousin, but the issue with Sarin was more pressing. "Today, I, um, I need to try and see Sarin."

"Isn't that dangerous considering Farrow's gunning for her?" Phoebe asked with a perplexed look in her eyes.

Meeting Sarin was risky, but she owed her friend more than just a phone call, and if her mother found them, she'd use her fire magic to protect her friend if necessary. "Maybe. But this can't wait."

"Well, if it's that important, I'm coming with you!" Phoebe proclaimed.

She stared into her cousin's soulful brown eyes. How could she let her down easily? "I think this is something I have to do alone."

"Why?" Phoebe snapped. "Why does everyone think I'm incapable of helping?"

A phantom wind blew through the kitchen in response to Phoebe's anger.

"That's not what I said," Faith responded in a calm voice, trying to diffuse the situation before her cousin's untrained magic turned on them both.

"Everyone treats me like I'm a child! Well, everyone but Selene, and now she's dead, so what am I supposed to do?"

A current of air whipped around her face. It was strong enough to ruffle her hair, but Phoebe didn't seem to notice.

"I don't think you're a child, but your emotions are getting the best of you right now! Just stop and take a breath!"

"Fuck that!" Phoebe yelled, slamming her hand down on the counter. "It's not fair!"

Another gust of wind blew through the kitchen with a force so strong it knocked her coffee mug right off the counter. Hitting the ground with an audible crack, the mug shattered into a dozen pieces. Glancing between the ruined mug and her cousin's face, she watched as the girl finally put the pieces together.

"Did....did I do that?" Phoebe asked in a shaky voice.

"I was wondering when you were going notice."

"What do you mean? I think I would know if my powers came in."

"I saw it yesterday at the funeral. You commanded the air, Phoebe. Your element is finally manifesting itself."

"But I wasn't even trying? And why is this happening now, after all this time?"

Faith had a few theories about that, but none of them were positive. "Do you really want my opinion?"

"I just asked for it, didn't I?" Phoebe snapped.

"First of all, stop with all the sarcasm. It isn't helping. We've all had our suspicions that our parents might be the ones stifling our powers, so what if that's true? My mom's been MIA. What if her lack of proximity to you unlocked whatever magical dampener she placed on you? Or maybe the grief over losing Selene was the catalyst you needed to jump-start your transition?"

Phoebe seemed dazed as she stared at the broken mug on the floor. "Both of those options suck. I'd rather have Selene than my magic."

"I know, Pheebs. But that's why you can't come with me to see Sarin. Your emotions are too volatile right now, and you don't know how to control your powers. I'm already risking a lot by going to see her in person and taking you with me puts us at added risk of exposure. What if you accidentally use your powers in public? I promise I'm not trying to treat you like a child. I just want Sarin to be safe, and I know you want the same thing."

"I get that, but what am I supposed to do while you're gone?"

"Stay inside the house and try to get a hold of your mom. She saw you use your power yesterday, too, but she didn't want to overwhelm you by bringing it up after the funeral. I think you two have a lot to talk about."

"Thanks for the toast, but I'm not hungry anymore."

She was about to tell her not to worry about it when Phoebe jumped up and wrapped her arms around her. The hug was sweet and unexpected, especially since Phoebe wasn't the touchy-feely type. Hugging her back, she felt the tears begin to swell. Lies and death had torn their family apart, and it was her job to put it back together, starting with Sarin. "I love you, Pheebs! And I want to tell you everything will be okay, but I'm not sure what that means anymore."

Pulling back, she looked at her cousin, really looked at her, and for the first time, she saw the strong, resilient woman Phoebe would one day become.

"Thank you for not sugarcoating any of this. I'm going to take your advice and call my mom. And for the record, I love you too, cuz."

After Phoebe left the room, she cleaned up the broken pieces of her favorite mug and poured herself a fresh cup of coffee. Her mother's secret was a game changer, and she had no idea how Sarin would react when she found out the truth. Grabbing her cell phone, she reminded herself to be strong as she called her best friend to work out the semantics of a face-to-face.

CHAPTER 14

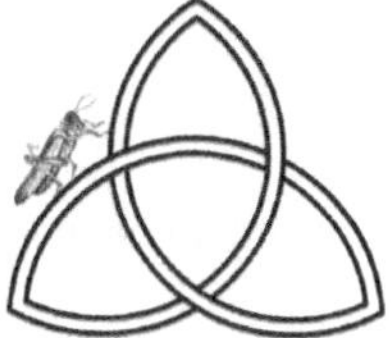

Sarin stood under the spray of the shower, letting the warm water calm the last of her raging nerves. The how's and the why's of the energy expulsion were still a mystery to her, but the heavy weight inside her chest felt lighter. Rinsing out her long, thick hair, she tried and subsequently failed to ignore the horrifying images of her mother's body lying inside a coffin. The idea that the person who'd brought her into this world was no longer a part of it was mind-bending and impossible to comprehend. She would never hear her mother's voice again or feel her warm embrace. A deep well of grief opened up in her heart, and when it threatened to drag her under, she turned the faucet to the cold setting in the hopes the freezing water would shock her back to the present. The frigid water had the desired effect, but she couldn't take it for long. Stepping out of the shower with a numbness that had nothing to do with the temperature, she towel-dried her wet hair, which was still full of conditioner. Drying off the rest of her body at an impressive speed, she pulled on the set of clothing Haven had left out for her and was surprised to find that everything fit. Glancing in the mirror, she blanched at the sight of her reflection. Hollow, vacant eyes stared back at her. Her haggard face was a testament to how quickly everything in life could change. Just days ago, she'd been carefree, enjoying nursing school, and now, her mother was dead, and she was hiding from a crazy, vengeful witch who wanted to murder her. If she survived this bullshit with Farrow, she had some serious soul-searching to do. She still wanted to pursue a career in medicine. That dream hadn't changed, but the nursing program had a strict attendance policy, and she knew it was only a matter of time before they officially kicked her out. Staring back at the reflection of the person who looked a lot like her old self, she vowed to try her best for today. That was all she could do. Sighing, she left the steam-filled bathroom to find Haven waiting for her by the front door.

"It's colder in the woods. Take this," Haven said as she handed her a thick wool-lined parka. "Are you wearing the bracelet?"

Holding up her arm, she revealed the small piece of jewelry Haven had spelled for her. "You said to keep it on at all times, and I'm listening."

Nodding, Haven opened the front door. "Good. And what do you do if Farrow finds us?"

Taking the coat, she shrugged into it before following Haven outside. The morning air smelled fresh and crisp. "I run and let you handle it."

As they walked deeper into the forest, Sarin was mesmerized by the beauty around them. The leaves seemed more vibrant, and the air smelled effervescent like the soil had just been tilled.

"Does this part of the forest always look like this?" she asked as she dragged her finger over the tip of an emerald-colored leaf.

Haven stopped short when a flock of birds exploded out of a nearby tree, and as they soared overhead, Sarin let out a gasp. She'd never seen birds like these before. Their feathers were a vibrant array of colors, and their golden beaks seemed to shimmer in the early morning sun.

"That's definitely not normal," Haven said, sounding as awestruck as Sarin felt.

Haven wanted to investigate this particular area of the forest before moving on to the clearing. So here they were, two freezing peas in a pod, exploring the unknown woods with zero direction. It all felt like a very bad idea. Following Haven down a winding path, Sarin heard the rush of water long before they stepped onto the lake's rocky shore. The turquoise basin that opened up at the end of the trail was breathtaking, but the roaring waterfall that cascaded down the side of the outcrops caught her attention the most. She'd lived in Canada most of her life, and gorgeous scenery like this never got old. Watching the water splash onto the glassy surface of the lake had a calming effect on her, and as Sarin breathed in the cool mountain air, she felt a sense of peace wash over her for the first time in a long time.

Haven's panicked scream pulled her back to the present, and when she turned around, she saw her cousin slowly backing away from the woods with her hands up in a defensive position. Following Haven's line of sight, she saw a white wolf emerge from behind the thick brush. It was huge and snarling at Haven, with a mouthful of oversized fangs that dripped with fresh blood. Sarin didn't know much about animals, but she knew enough to know that wolves didn't have six pairs of canine teeth. The white-haired beast was twice the size of a normal wolf and had large, intelligent eyes that glowed with an unnatural yellow sheen. Rearing back on its hind legs, it leaped at Haven. Time seemed to stand still as she stood on the banks of the lake, feeling helpless to do anything but watch the horrific scene play out before her. Haven flickered her wrists, sending two thick shards of ice racing through the air. The first one missed, but the second one hit its mark, stabbing the animal right in the face. The wolf let out a loud howl of pain before landing in a bloodied heap at the base of Haven's feet.

Running for her cousin, she was ashamed that she'd been momentarily frozen by fear. "What is that? Are you okay?"

Haven's frantic gaze moved back and forth between her hands and the dead beast in front of her. "I can't wield ice. Something's wrong."

No shit, Sarin thought. A monster wolf had just attacked her. Its snow-white face was now a mask of scarlet and gore, but Sarin still nudged it with her boot to make sure it was dead.

"I froze. I'm sorry," she admitted.

Haven stared at her hands like she didn't know who they belonged to. "I barely had time to react, and you were twenty feet away. Don't beat yourself up about it. I'm fine."

Her cousin didn't look fine, but she kept that little comment to herself. Circling the wolf's carcass, she noticed the animal's legs were covered in thick brown vines. Crouching down, she tried to pull one of the vines off, but to her shock, she realized they were a part of the animal itself.

"Did you see its eyes?" Haven asked in a shaky voice. "They were glowing."

"I did, and they were unnerving. What do you think happened to it?"

Sitting down on the rocky shore, Haven wrapped her arms around herself. "I think whatever's inside that clearing is affecting the land and animals and changing them somehow. But the real question is, why? And is there anything we can do about it?"

Sarin sat down beside her. "What about your powers?"

Haven held out her palm, and a ball of fire appeared in the center of it. Extinguishing it, she repeated the action, and the flames appeared once again. Sarin was mesmerized as she watched the flames dance in the frigid morning breeze. "It looks like my magic is back to normal, but I've never been able to create ice before. If the magical disturbances are coming from inside the clearing, I'm not sure it's safe to train there. Maybe we should train here instead?"

The wolf's body began to decompose before their very eyes, and within seconds, its entire body had disintegrated into nothing but a pile of dried bones and ash.

"Well, I take that back!" Haven proclaimed as she jumped to her feet. "I'll take my chances in the clearing over that shit!"

Scrambling after her cousin, Sarin was happy to put some distance between herself and what remained of the wolf. The strange happenings inside these woods seemed like a total contradiction. The birds and trees had been transformed into something beautiful, almost ethereal, while the wolf had been transformed into a horrific, nightmarish creature. Sarin wondered how the magic from the clearing, if that's what was causing it, was choosing or if there was a bigger, more malevolent hand guiding it all.

•••

Sarin stayed just outside the clearing as she waited for Haven's instruction. She knew Haven wanted to try to contact her mother again after they trained, but she had no interest in being sucked into that weird empty place again.

"Are you sure you're up for training?" Haven asked as she shucked out of her leather jacket. "I know I've been pushing its importance, but that shit with the wolf was intense."

She wasn't sure of anything anymore, but she followed Haven's lead and ditched her parka. "I don't think we have a choice. Like you said before, if we keep waiting, one of us is likely to end up dead."

"Then let's get started," Haven announced as she began to slowly circle her.

"As a spirit witch, you should be able to access and control another person's soul. That light bomb you shot off inside the cabin is a powerful weapon, and you've already seen what can happen if you let it get on top of you. But once you learn to harness it, you should essentially be able to control another person. For today, I want to focus on defensive magic. If you can't protect yourself, then this is all for nothing, right? One of the first steps in practicing magic is to master visualization. This technique works for everyone, regardless of your specific power or element. Visualizing your magic as a tangible thing makes it easier to control. Are you ready?"

Sarin blanched. "Ready for what?"

BEEP BEEP BEEP

Covering her ears, she doubled over as the blaring noise rang out inside her ears. She couldn't think much less act.

BEEP BEEP BEEP

"Make it stop!" she screamed over the raging crescendo that threatened to rupture her eardrums.

"Stop it yourself!" Haven yelled back.

Sarin tried to think, to focus, but the ear-splitting racket was relentless.

BEEP BEEP BEEP

On and on it went. Dropping to her knees, she grunted in pain. She'd do anything to make it stop.

VISUALIZE

The word was a soft whisper in the back of her turbulent mind. In between choppy breaths, Sarin closed her eyes and tried to do what Haven asked of her. Picturing the deafening sound as an actual shape, she molded it into a square and then visualized herself wrapping it in a soundproof blanket. To her surprise and amazement, the noise stopped completely.

Cracking her eyes open, she was annoyed to find Haven looking over at her with a huge shit-eating grin plastered across her face. "Not bad, cousin. Not bad."

"You couldn't have warned me first?" she snapped, shaking her head to try and get rid of the residual ringing in her ears, Sarin.

Haven's expression turned serious. "I asked you if you were ready, and that's far more than the enemy will offer you."

Sarin didn't want to admit it, but her cousin was right.

"I don't know about you, but I could really use a beer."

She was proud of her accomplishment, but she knew damn well that she had a lot more to learn. "That's all the training you want to do?"

"No, but you exceeded my expectations for day one, and since you just had an unprecedented magical eruption less than twenty-four hours ago, I don't want to push our luck. Tomorrow's another story."

Walking over to pick up the parka she'd left on top of a fallen log, she noticed something shiny sticking out from underneath it. Reaching down to pick it up, she gasped in shock when she realized what it was.

Haven must have felt her trepidation because she was by her side a second later. "What is it?"

She swallowed as she took in the sight of the familiar gold necklace that housed a beautiful turquoise pendant. "This is Farrow's, and she never takes it off. It was a special gift from Faith."

"Shit!" Haven announced. "That means she's been here."

Pulling her away from the clearing with lightning speed, Haven ushered them back through the woods. "We need to get back to the cabin in case she's still in the area."

"What if she's watching us right now?" Sarin asked as a feeling of dread washed over her.

"Then I suggest we run."

•••

Thirty minutes and a whole lot of sweat later, Sarin sat on the couch next to Haven with an ice-cold lemonade in her hand and a sharp cramp in her side. She hated sports, and their little sprint through the woods highlighted her lack of cardiovascular training. Haven was nursing a beer and flipping through the channels on the old-school cable box when she saw Korynn Miller's stupid face fill the screen.

"Hey, can you pause for a second?"

The local news station was doing a segment on downtown Huntsville, and Sarin cringed at the sight of her high school nemesis.

"I take it she's not your bestie?" Haven questioned with a smirk.

"Yeah, no! She's the biggest drama queen in town and a total B."

The headline at the bottom of the screen read: *Local town terrorized by rabid animals.*

Korynn's eyes filled with tears as she told the reporter all about her near-death experience with what she could only describe as a rabid Lynx with glowing red eyes. Apparently, her boyfriend had been taken to the hospital after sustaining a bite wound while trying to protect her. If she hadn't seen the mutated wolf with her own eyes, she wouldn't have given Korynn's story much weight, but the attacks were too similar to ignore.

The landline let out a loud shrill, and Sarin jumped at the sound. There was only one person who had this number, so she wasn't surprised to hear Faith's voice on the other end of the line. Her friend was frantic and crying.

"Slow down, Faith. Okay, okay, yeah, I'll figure something out. I need to talk to you, too. Just calm down, okay? I'll meet you there as soon as I can. Faith?"

The line went dead.

"Being around Faith is dangerous," Haven warned. "Are you sure this in-person meeting is worth it?"

"You should have heard her, Haven. She's scared, and the cabin line just went dead, so I have no way to call her back. I appreciate everything you've done for me, but I can't leave my friend high and dry. Especially after what she did for my mom."

Haven tossed her the keys to the borrowed car. "Fine. But you're driving, and don't take that bracelet off under any circumstances."

"Really? Just like that? You're not going to give me a big speech or tie me down to a chair?"

"I don't like this plan, but I understand why you need to go, and I can't let you go alone," Haven stated as she placed her half-empty beer down on the coffee table.

"But Sarin, if Farrow finds us, the same rules apply. You have to run. You're not ready to face her yet, and I can buy us some time if push comes to shove. Promise me?"

"I promise," Sarin vowed, knowing full well she would never willingly leave her cousin behind to fight her fight.

CHAPTER 15

Dusk settled over downtown Huntsville as Sarin parked the car in front of Mills. The dim glow of the streetlamps cast strange shadows on the buildings, and she felt a sense of unease wash over her as she scooped out her surroundings. Haven was passed out next to her in the passenger seat, and she didn't have the heart to wake her. Her cousin had been nodding off during the first half of the drive, and it had taken a lot of clever convincing to get her to succumb to the sleep she so desperately needed. Sarin had promised to wake her up once they arrived, but now, starting over at her as she softly snored, she wasn't sure she should. It was clear that Haven hadn't slept in days, and if her body was at its breaking point, then the least Sarin could do was give her a few more minutes to rest. The River Front was only a few feet away, and if she was being honest, she really wanted to talk to Faith alone. Leaving the car running, she left her cousin to sleep and quickly locked the door behind her.

"Hey, stranger," the familiar voice called out, catching her off guard.

Alex was walking up the stairs that led to the River Front, looking just as sexy as he always did, but tonight, something about his posture seemed off. Alex had a natural stride that screamed *I'm causal and relaxed*, but today, his back was ramrod straight, and every muscle in his body seemed tense. He'd been texting her non-stop lately, but she'd been too preoccupied with her own shit to respond. As he approached her, a sense of hostility skittered over her skin. The feeling didn't make any sense. She had no reason to fear Alex, but all her instincts screamed *DANGER!*

Plastering a fake smile on her face, she tried to act casual. "Are you leaving or just getting to work?"

The air around Alex seemed to ripple as he closed the last few feet between them. His ordinarily handsome face, now illuminated by the streetlights, emphasized his hallowed-out eyes and sallow-looking skin. Sarin swallowed hard as she realized something was very wrong with him. Taking in the sight of his sickly pallor, she wondered if the magic from the forest had infected him somehow, like the animals.

Alex grinned at her with an unsettling familiarity. "The owner asked me to stop by and turn off a few things she forgot about. She decided to close the bar early tonight after hearing about that crazy animal attack on the news."

Her palms began to sweat as her senses went on high alert. "You really should be getting home, Alex. It's not safe out here."

"I think you should take your own advice," he countered. "Where have you been, by the way? I stopped by your house a few times to check in on you, but you haven't been home."

The last time she'd seen Alex, they had parted on good terms, but they weren't on *a let's check in on each other level*. The idea that he was actively looking for her gave her the creeps.

"That's kind of you. I've just been really busy," she lied, inching her way toward the safety of the car. "And I don't mean to be rude, but I really have to go. Why don't we try and catch-up next week sometime?"

"I'm sure you can spare a few minutes for an old flame?" Alex asked in a mocking tone.

Turning around, she fumbled with the door handle. "That was a long time ago, Alex, and if you remember correctly, we just became friends, so don't go and fuck it up now by being an asshole."

Alex didn't respond with words, but she saw him lunge for her in the reflection of the side-view mirror. Spinning around, she raised her hands in anticipation of the attack and was surprised when a stream of white-hot energy filled her hands. Her magic had answered the call and was waiting for her to command it. Too bad Alex was human, and she'd just magically outed herself. She didn't want to hurt him, but he didn't seem like himself right now. Consequences be damned.

The light made him pause, but the evil smile that spread across his face made her blood run cold. "That little trick didn't hold me for long last time, witch!"

As the cruel words washed over her, a horrible realization dawned. This wasn't Alex. The doppelgänger had come back and assumed Alex's form, which could only mean one thing - Alex was dead. The pause of realization cost her, and before she had time to react, the doppelgänger grabbed her by the shoulders and shoved her to the ground. Straddling her, it pinned her in place by positioning its knees on top of her arms, and as its fetid breath washed over her, she tried not to vomit.

"Now, it's time to finish this," it taunted in Alex's voice.

Sarin retreated into herself as the doppelgänger pummeled its fists into her face. Pain exploded behind her eyes before branching out across her face as she took hit after hit. She couldn't see her hands to know if her light was still active, but it didn't matter; she couldn't use her power against the doppelgänger if she couldn't lift her arms. This was it, game over. In the midst of the agony and random flashes of light that flickered behind her closed eyes, she felt like giving up. Why prolong the inevitable when there was just more pain and heartache to come? But then a warm voice called out to her from somewhere in the darkness. It was a familiar voice she thought she'd never hear again.

"Remember what you are." It was her mother's voice.

What did that mean? She had no time to ponder it, no time to think. There was just the crunch of her nose breaking and a warm trickle as blood came spilling down her face.

*"Spirit Witch! "H*er mother's voice screamed.

Hadn't Haven told her that spirit witches could control souls? She couldn't defend herself with her body, but maybe she could fight the doppelgänger with her spirit. She had no idea how to access that part of her power, but at that moment, some primal part of her, desperate to survive, sprung to life. Looking with her magic and not her eyes, she scanned the doppelgänger's body, searching for its spirit, soul, or anything to latch on to, but all she found was an empty husk. Pushing further into its essence, she kept searching until she saw what her brain could only describe as a group of dancing shadows hidden deep within the recess of the monster's mind. Homing in on the black wraiths, she was horrified when she realized the shadows weren't dancing at all. No, the inky masses were writhing and undulating in pain. Moving closer, she realized the shadows were all echoes of the doppelgänger's victims, who were silently screaming as they relived the moment the monster stole their last breaths and assumed their likeness. Their memories had been stored away in this place like ghastly statutes on a trophy shelf. A small piece of her mother, Selene, and Alex all lingered here. As she approached them, they parted to reveal a golden pedestal with a folder of paper sitting on top of it. At least, that's what her mind perceived it to be. It was something the doppelgänger didn't want her to find. Something the echoes were leading her to.

*"Its name! "*They whispered in unison.

"Call out its name!" They urged.

She didn't know if the corrupted magic from the clearing was responsible for what was happening to her or if this was all her doing, but as the echoes encouraged her, she moved closer to the pedestal until she was standing right in front of it. Reaching down, she picked up the folder piece of paper. Forcing herself out of the monster's mind, she reoriented herself back in her body as a new wave of pain and nausea washed over her. Bucking under the weight of the doppelgänger, she tried with all her remaining strength to get it off of her. She needed to take a breath. Just one breath would be enough for her to call out its name. It laughed at her as she flailed around, but her plan worked, and when it shifted its weight to try and pin her down again, she gasped.

A sharp stabbing pain erupted inside her chest as she choked out the one name that could save her. "Abyssal!"

The pounding on her face eased.

"How?" the doppelgänger demanded with a strangled cry.

Cracking open her swollen left eye, she saw the look of shock that bloomed across its blurry, hateful face as its body began to convulse over hers in a stream of erratic movements. Shoving off of her, it began clawing at its own face. Alex's human features slowly melted away to reveal the true face of the creature she'd accidentally created. The thing before her had thick grey-colored skin and elongated spindly appendages that ended in curved blackened claws. Its humanoid-shaped head was oval and bald, and as it stared over at her with a mouth full of shark-like teeth, its onyx-colored eyes radiated pure hatred. Meeting the monster stare for stare, she felt a sense of satisfaction as she watched its skin turn an oily shade of black before its entire body exploded into a pile of ash. She couldn't move, so she stayed on the ground, as ash rained down on her like the cruel summer rain. The twisted reflection of her past mistake was gone, but so was Alex. The clicking of shoes on the pavement made her tense up, but when Faith's blonde hair bounced into view, she relaxed a little.

"Sarin? Sarin? Oh my god, what happened to your face?"

She tried to speak through her swollen lips, but the words sounded jumbled as a fresh gush of blood came out instead. All that remained of the doppelgänger was a steaming pile of embers and ash.

"Doppel...." she tried to explain, but there was too much blood in her mouth. The blood burned her throat as it went back down, and she knew she was in serious need of medical attention.

Faith jumped at the sound of a car door shutting behind them.

"What the hell, Sarin! You were supposed to wake me up!" Haven yelled as she rushed over to her.

Sarin opened her mouth to say I'm sorry, but all that came out was another stream of blood. God, she was tired, so very tired.

Haven crouched in front of her and lightly brushed the bloodied hair away from her face. "Don't pass out on me, Sarin. This is going to hurt, but I promise it will all be over soon."

Haven's voice sounded far away as she began chanting. Sarin tried to hang on to her cousin's words, but when her face erupted in a fresh wave of unbearable pain, she passed out instead. Unfortunately for her, she came to a few seconds later when her nose shifted back in place with an audible crunch. The sound made her stomach roll with nausea, but after a few more grueling seconds, the pain finally began to ebb, and she was able to blink open both of her eyes.

"Good as new," Haven announced with a warm smile.

Running her hands over her cheeks and mouth, Sarin was amazed to find that they were back to normal. Staring over at the pile of ash, she felt vindicated in destroying the creature that had taken the lives of her mother, Selene, and Alex. Three lives had been taken from this world because of her carelessness, and she could never repay that debt, but at least the monster was gone.

Faith sat beside her. "What happened?"

Sarin's eyes filled with tears as she explained how Alex, aka the doppelgänger, had gotten the drop on her.

"I worked with him and didn't know," Faith added in a defeated voice. "How is that possible?"

"Doppelgänger's have access to the memories of the bodies they steal, remember? It knew everything about Alex. More than enough to assume his life and make you believe the lie."

"Did you take off your bracelet?" Haven asked as she scanned the darkened streets.

"No," Sarin admitted, pointing to her wrist where the bracelet remained intact.

"Well, shit! I don't know if the doppelgänger was immune to my protection spell or if my magic is being corrupted again." Haven said absently. "You did well, cousin, but you didn't wake me up like you promised. I should never have fallen asleep in the first place, but from here on out, you need to keep your promises. If Farrow had shown up in the middle of that fight with the doppelgänger, you'd be dead!"

Haven was right. Her choice to let her sleep had been the wrong call.

"We need to get out of the open. Faith, can you help me get her to the car?"

"I still need to talk to you about something," Faith said as she helped Sarin stand up.

"Can you tell her at the cabin?" Haven interjected. "No offense, but I don't trust your mother. We found her necklace in the woods earlier today, so I know she's hiding close by."

"Shit!" Faith exclaimed. "She didn't come home this morning, and I'm worried that whatever she's planning might be coming to a head!"

"All the more reason to get your ass in the car and talk to Sarin later!" Haven called out as she slid into the driver's seat. "And turn your cell phone off before you leave this parking lot."

Nodding, Faith opened the passenger side door to help Sarin inside. "I'll follow you."

One threat had been dismantled, but Sarin wasn't sure she had the strength to hurt anyone else, let alone Faith's mother.

CHAPTER 16

Faith was sweating despite the evening chill as she parked her car in the gravel-lined driveway behind Haven's. She'd gone to Mills with the sole purpose of telling Sarin what she'd learned, only to find her friend hurt and bleeding. Her first thought had been - *thank god it wasn't at the hands of my mother*. Sarin had come out on top, but Faith still felt guilty for not getting there in time to help her. When she found Sarin lying on the ground in a pool of her own blood, her mind had gone to a dark place. Her best friend's cheek had been split open down to the bone, and the rest of her face resembled a swollen mask of blood and gore. If it hadn't been for Haven, Sarin would've needed some serious reconstructive surgery to fix all the damage the doppelgänger inflicted on her. The healing spell Haven had performed on Sarin's face was a miracle in itself.

Sitting behind the wheel, Faith switched off her headlights as she watched Haven help Sarin to the front door. Taking a deep breath, she tried to prepare herself for the difficult conversation with Sarin when a blur of motion outside the passenger window caught her attention. Something big was pacing back and forth near the tree line to the left of the cabin. It looked like an animal in the darkness, but something about the way it moved made the hair on her arms stand on end. It didn't help her unease when she saw Haven motioning for her to come to them with frantic waves of her hands. Unbuckling her seatbelt, she jumped out of the driver's side seat and rushed toward the cabin. The low warning growl made her pause.

"Walk faster, and if something comes at you, blast it with your fire," Haven called out with a tinge of panic in her voice.

"I don't want to hurt an animal," she stated, picking up the pace.

"I'm not sure that *is* an animal," Sarin shouted. "Hurry!"

Her anxiety rose to full-on panic as the growling gained in volume.

"Run!" Haven yelled. "Now!"

The shadow darted out of the woods and tackled her before she could take another step. Rolling on the ground, she managed to kick off whatever it was before landing on her ass in the grassy lawn beside the cabin. The shadow stood with its back to her, and at that moment, she realized with chilling clarity that Sarin was right. It wasn't an animal. As the thing before her straightened, she noticed its body resembled that of a woman's, but the rest of it looked like a nightmarish mix of plant and animal.

It turned around and looked at her, and that's when Faith lost all sense of reality. "Mom?" she gasped. Is that really you?"

"You're not supposed to be here," the beast before her crooned in an otherworldly-sounding voice.

She couldn't move, couldn't breathe, as she took in the sight of the thing that had once been her mother.

"What happened to you?" her brain was having a hard time processing what she was seeing. How could this monstrous thing be her mother?

The beast's fawn-like face looked like an elongated replica of her mother's, but everything else had been altered. Horns protruded from the sides of her head, and her body, oh god, her body! It looked like it was made from nothing but twisted bark and vines. Her mother's new set of eyes was probably the most unnerving of all. They were round and owl-like, and their once warm hazel color had been replaced by a bright shade of yellow that glowed in the darkness. Locking eyes with her mother, Faith shuddered under her predatory gaze.

Tilting her head in a very birdlike way, her mother issued a warning. "You should run. You're not the one it wants."

She had no idea what her mother was talking about, but standing on shaky legs, she squared her shoulders. "If you want to hurt Sarin, you'll have to go through me first."

"Very well." her mother taunted as she reached out and grabbed her by the neck. "You should have stayed away from that little bitch like I told you to; then, this wouldn't be happening."

Faith's throat burned as her mother's vine-like fingers dug in harder.

"If you had told me the truth, I could have helped you. We could have stopped whatever this is." The words came out as a strangled cry.

Farrow smiled, flashing her massive set of canines. "Too little, too late."

A combination of light and heat came out of nowhere, blasting Farrow in the back.

Howling in outrage, she let go of Faith to confront her attackers, and that's when Faith noticed Sarin and Haven running towards her, screaming for her to get out of the way.

"Stop!" Faith screamed in protest. "Don't hurt her!"

Farrow howled again, and the sound was guttural and animalistic.

Sarin didn't stop; instead, she struck Farrow with another blast of her energy power. The force of the shock wave pushed Farrow closer to the woods, and as she retreated under the canopy of trees, she paused to peg Faith with one last look of warning before she disappeared completely. The world began to twinkle in and out of Faith's line of vision, but then

Sarin was there, placing her shoulder underneath her arm and ushering her across the lawn.

Haven's hands were noticeably shaking as she opened the door to the cabin. "What was that thing? What the fuck happened to her?"

"She's a Dryad," Sarin responded, all matter-of-factly.

"A what?" Faith demanded as they rushed inside the safety of the cabin. "How do you know that?"

"You're bleeding," Sarin announced as she forced her to sit down on the couch. "It looks like one of her claws nicked your neck. Haven, get the first aid kit!"

Grabbing Sarin by the shoulder, she forced her to look her in the eyes. "I don't care about the scratch, Sarin. How do you know what my mother is?"

Sarin gently shrugged her off. "When my energy ball hit her, the word rang out inside my mind. I think killing the doppelgänger opened up some magical well of power inside me."

After delivering the first aid kit, Haven paced back and forth in front of the couch, tapping her chin with her index finger. "I think it's all connected. The power around your mother felt polluted, just like the magic that's been changing the plants and animals."

"So how do we help her?" she asked in a strangled voice.

"I'm not sure we can," Haven said with a heavy sigh. "We need to cut off the tainted magic coming from inside that clearing. If we can do that, maybe we have a shot at helping your mom."

Faith's head was spinning. "We need to go back to my house. My aunt Fallon can help us."

"We will, but you need to rest and let me put a bandage on your neck first," Sarin interjected in a calm voice. "It's late, and I don't think Farrow's coming back tonight."

Faith questioned whether telling them what she'd learned was a good idea right now. Haven was a scared, jittery mess, and Sarin, god help her, had just gone through her own traumatic experience with the doppelgänger. No, she decided. Now wasn't the right time to burden them with the truth. She would tell them tomorrow.

Trying to change the subject, she asked, "Sarin, can I see the necklace you found?"

Reaching into her pocket, Sarin handed over the gold trinket, and when Faith realized which one it was, her eyes misted. She'd given this particular necklace to her mother five years ago on her birthday, and she never took it off. The fact that it had been discarded out in those woods like a piece of trash was telling. As was the monumental realization that her mother had been transformed into some kind of mutated forest monster. Or Dryad. Whatever the hell that was. It was strange, but a small part of her felt better knowing that her mother was an actual monster instead of just some run-of-the-mill psychopath. Putting the necklace around her neck, she leaned into Sarin and let her tears fall. They were tears over the loss of her mother and tears for all the heartache still to come.

CHAPTER 17

Haven closed herself inside her bedroom to give the girls some privacy. They needed some time alone together, and her restlessness wasn't helping. That Dryad scared the shit out of her, and that was saying something considering all the monsters she'd encountered in her short lifetime. Whatever was lying in wait inside the clearing had the power to alter matter on a fundamental level, and that knowledge shook her to the core. She needed to find a way to stop Farrow and stuff all that corrupted magic back where it had come from. In her past experience, the steps had always been the same. Research the enemy, come up with a game plan, and then be prepared to say fuck it all when the actual shit hits the fan. This time, she wanted an easier solution. Luckily, she now had access to an ancient vessel of information that was as old as magic itself. Lying back on her bed, she mouthed the words to the familiar spell that would send her consciousness into the ether. If there was anyone who could give her the answers she needed, it was Lucifer. The sensation of leaving her body felt normal, but everything that came after was anything but. She'd been aiming for Lucifer's private chamber. The one she'd been to before, but when she opened her eyes, she found herself far from his sanctuary's warm, glowing interior. The landscape surrounding her now was more on brand with what she imagined Hell to be. Technically, Lucifer's chamber was also in Hell, so maybe she'd just missed the mark. The scenery before her was empty and barren, just like the place the clearing had sent her to. Maybe she wasn't in Hell at all, after all? Maybe her magic had gone rogue on her again and sent her back to that place. Instead of ending the spell and returning back to the cabin right then and there, she let her curiosity get the best of her.

This place held an eerie, smoky haze, and the path before her was lined with barren trees on both sides. Their twisted branches formed strange shapes that looked a hell of a lot like human bodies. The bark was charred to a black crisp, and as she stepped in closer, the tree on her right moaned. *MOANED!* Jumping back, she was sickened by the grotesqueness of it all. These trees didn't just look like people; they were actual fucking people! The branches were made of human limbs that had been disjointed and elongated, and the trucks were nothing but a pile of charred body parts stacked one on top of the other. The disgusting smell of sulfur turned her stomach sour as she maneuvered herself through the sea of people trees. Covering her mouth with her hands, she was careful not to touch any of them. This place had to be Hell. How was she supposed to fix anything if her magic kept screwing with her? The little mishap with the ice and the wolf had worked out in her favor, but teleporting herself to an unknown location was downright dangerous.

In the distance, several shapes sat clustered together in a tight-knit circle. The unidentified forms writhed and undulated around something large that was lying on the ground in the middle of them. Inching her way closer to get a better view, she froze as recognition dawned. Huddled together, in a mass of wings and fangs, were a blood-thirsty group of Harpies. She only knew them for what they were because one of her former allies had been one himself. The hideous creatures had long, crooked beaks, emaciated hollow bodies, and black oily wings that looked bat-like. Panic washed over her as she realized she'd teleported herself into the seventh circle of Hell. This was The Vile Wood, the resting place for all the souls on Earth who committed suicide. At the sound of her sharp inhale, six pairs of beady yellow eyes turned to stare at her, with gaping maws full of blood and gore. Stretching to their full height, the Harpies left their lifeless prey where it was and set their predatory gazes on her. Swallowing, she jumped when the one on the far left smiled at her. She had no idea how something with a beak could form a fucking smile, but the effect was terrifying.

Her plan was to firebomb them all, but when she reached for her power, nothing happened. Not even a tiny spark lit inside her hand. Helpless and on the verge of hysterics, she turned around and ran. The human trees began to move, uprooting themselves and lurching for her on their blackened roots that now resembled clawed bony feet. Seconds later, she was caged in by their human-like branches, a helpless meal for the hungry beasts chasing her. The Harpies moved swiftly, snapping their beaks and squawking until only feet separated them. The inhuman roar that rang out was so loud that it shook the ground, and to her surprise, the Harpies retreated in the opposite direction. Wrenching herself free of the trees, she turned toward the source of the sound with trepidation. Whatever was coming for her was far worse than the Harpies. The human trees teetered their way back to their posts to let a different kind of monster through. The beast raced toward her with glowing crimson-colored eyes and a look of absolute rage plastered across his too handsome face. Lucifer was here, and as he embraced her, everything went dark.

Pinpricks of light passed through Haven's closed lids as she heard Lucifer's pissed-off ranting. "Stupid, stupid, little witch!"

"Insults aren't helping!" she shot back as she took in her new surroundings.

This cozy living space had been her aim from the start. The warm fire burning in the oversized hearth was welcoming, and the leather couch she was lying on felt like smooth silk underneath her fingers. This posh, sophisticated lounge was a total contradiction to the brutal, hellish landscape just outside these walls. Pushing herself to a seated position, she noted the grim expression on Lucifer's face as he flexed and un-flexed his claw-tipped hands.

"Why would you project yourself into the Vile Wood?" he accused in a vicious tone.

If he'd been a second later, she would've been ripped to shreds.

Not wanting to give him the satisfaction of a thank you right now, she rolled her eyes. "Maybe I thought it would be a nice vacation from the magical crisis I'm currently in. Or maybe, I wanted to offer myself up as a sacrifice, so I never have to find out what your plans for me really are."

He was clearly not amused. Crossing his arms over his chest, he continued to glare at her.

Throwing her hands up in frustration, she huffed. "Obviously, that location wasn't my goal, but my magic is totally fucked right now!"

"And why is that?" he demanded, still fuming.

His posture was unyielding and taut, and god help her, he looked sexy, all riled up and angry.

"Oh, I don't know, maybe because there's some magical force hidden in the woods where my mother grew up that's infecting the land and changing things. Like my magic, animals, and people."

Saying it out loud made her sound insane. But then she reminded herself she was in Hell and sitting across from Lucifer himself, so nothing was truly unhinged anymore. "I came here to ask if you know anything about Dryads. This magical infection, or whatever it is, turned my friend's mother into one, and I needed information. Since you've been around since the literal dawn of time, I thought you might have some insight."

Ignoring her question, Lucifer walked over to his exquisitely embellished bar and poured himself a glass of amber-colored liquid. He swirled the liquid around in the glass for a few seconds before taking a long sip. Picking up a second glass, he gestured toward her, but she declined. She needed a clear head right now, especially when she was in such close proximity to him.

Leaning against the bar, he continued to sip his drink in silence.

"Well?" she snapped. "I guess this was all a big waste of time. I'll be leaving now."

"Relax! I'm thinking. It's been a long time since I've thought about any of the so-called Gods that used to roam this Earth, so give me a minute."

The way he said *this Earth* made her feel funny. Like, were there other Earths? Those were big questions for another time.

"You already know this, but when the angels brought magic to your world during the Fall, some of that magic infused with humans, creating the first magic wielders you now call Witches. But the truth is, the Earth held its own magic long before we arrived. An old, ancient magic that's vastly different from what's been ingrained into your DNA."

She was officially intrigued.

"I've only encountered one Dryad in my time, and it was just in passing."

Pausing, he took another long sip of his drink. "When I Fell, I was only on Earth for a short time before God sent me here to serve my penance. The Earth was young then, primal, and full of creatures you've only heard about in Lore. The Dryad I encountered was an Earth elemental who had power over flora and fauna. She was timid and kind. A keeper of the land."

A picture of Farrow's contorted face flashed inside her mind. She was horrific and terrifying and the farthest thing from a kind keeper of the land.

"That's not what Farrow has become. Whatever created her turned her into a vengeful monster. Or maybe her twisted soul did that on its own."

"There's a book in my private library that might be of help."

Haven shivered as she recalled the last time she'd been forced to use a page from one of his books. That page had come from his Dark Book, and its parchment had been so evil that it burned on contact.

"Not that book," he interjected, reading her thoughts as usual.

"Great. Can we go get it now?"

Pushing himself off the bar, he stalked toward her. "It's not that easy, my little witch. The place where it's stored is not a place you want to visit, especially after your little jaunt to The Vile Wood. No, this is something I have to retrieve on my own."

She hated how much his nearness affected her. Her entire body was buzzing with excitement. "I'll just sit here and hold my breath until you come back."

Shaking his head, he sighed. "Your real body isn't here, so if I hand the book to you, it will remain here when you poof back home."

"Then how is this helpful?" she spat. "I need answers now!"

"Do you trust anyone?" he crooned in a voice that was far too sexy.

She answered him honestly, "No, I don't! Not after the last two years of my life."

"I hope to change that one day. The book is gold and decorated in filigree and believe me when I say you'll know it when you see it."

His response was confusing. "If you're going to teleport it to me at the cabin, then why do I need help recognizing it?"

The arrogant smile he flashed her was annoying. "I have to send the book to a place with consecrated ground. There's an old library just outside of town that fits the bill. It was built on the site of an old church, and bonus points; it holds a collection of rare books. It's the closest place I can send it, but Haven, you have to act quickly. I don't know how the book will react if the magical infection you speak of reaches it. Like most things in Hell, the book is alive in the sense that it has sentience."

"Great. That's just what we need, a possessed book running around on the loose! Will I be able to with me, or does it have to stay there?"

Sitting next to her on the sofa, Lucifer lounged back like he didn't have a care in the world. And as she took in the striking sight of him, she supposed he didn't. He was trapped inside Hell for all eternity, so why should any problems up top affect him?

"I have to send it there, but once you retrieve it, it can leave the grounds. It's the best I can do for now. Take it or leave it, but the book will be waiting for you in the morning at Raven's Repository."

She was grateful for his help, but one compelling question still lingered in her mind.

"I have another request before I go. Can you stop being so cryptic and just tell me what you want from me? All this waiting for you to come clean is extremely aggravating."

He looked her up and down, and the rim around his onyx-colored eyes blazed a bright shade of crimson.

"You want honesty, and I respect that, but you're not ready to hear the truth. Once your Dryad situation is resolved, we can talk. Until then, I wish you well, my little witch."

Taking her hand in his, he pressed his lips against her knuckles as her spirit was whisked back to the cabin.

Haven's heart was racing as she slammed back into her body, and the sensation had nothing to do with the astral projection spell and everything to do with the hungry look in Lucifer's eyes as she left him.

CHAPTER 18

Faith woke up in a weird position. It was a testament to the stress she'd been under that she'd slept at all. Sarin was still asleep on the other end of the sofa, dead to the world. Her mouth was dry, and her head was pounding, two telltale signs of an oncoming migraine. The horrifying image of her mother towering before her in full Dryad form flashed through her mind, and her head throbbed in response. Farrow hadn't seemed scared by her transformation, but something in Faith's gut told her that becoming a Dryad wasn't what her mother had bargained for.

"Penny for your thoughts?"

She jumped at the sound of Haven's voice. She hadn't noticed her lingering in the bedroom doorway. "They might cost you a million dollars at this point! There are so many of them."

Haven chuckled at her retort, and the sound was strangely comforting. "When are you planning to tell her the truth?"

Her heart began to race at the accusation. How could Haven possibly know the secret she was keeping? "What are you talking about?"

Haven motioned for her to come into her room. "You do realize that one of my powers is telepathy, right? It comes and goes, so I can't decipher exactly what you're hiding, but your mind is screaming that we're all related somehow, and I can feel your apprehension about telling Sarin. Care to elaborate?"

Wiping her sweaty palms off on her jeans, she left Sarin to sleep and followed Haven into the bedroom. Shutting the door behind them, she sat down at the end of Haven's bed because her legs felt like they might give out on her otherwise. "I wanted to tell her last night, but it felt too heavy after everything."

Leaning back against the closed door, Haven absently picked at her nails. "I know you want to protect her, but we don't know jack shit about what's really going on in that clearing or what it did to your mother. So, any information you have might mean life or death."

She sucked in a deep breath before blurting out the big family secret. "We're cousins. As in the three of us."

To her surprise, Haven didn't completely freak out. "You already know?"

"No. But I have a strong connection with Sarin, and when you're around, I feel the same way about you. It didn't make sense to me at first, and I didn't have much time to mull it over with all the crazy shit going on."

Nerves were making Faith all jittery, and she couldn't stop bouncing her foot up and down. "The truth affects you too, not just her."

Pushing herself off the door, Haven came over to sit beside her on the bed, "I'm here, and I'm listening."

She wanted to tell Haven everything, but the words got stuck inside her throat.

"I know you're nervous," Haven prompted with a warm smile, "but I promise you I can handle whatever you're about to drop on me. Nothing you can say would shock me after the last few years of my life."

She wasn't sure if she agreed with her. "How much did Sarin tell you about my family?"

"Not much. We've been a little distracted since we met."

Haven's voice was even and calm, and Faith knew she was trying to make this safe space for her to share.

"You want the Cliff Notes version? My aunt Fallon and I found a journal documenting our family history, and in it, my mother claims that your mother and Sarin's father are her siblings."

The look of shock that bloomed across Haven's face was the reaction she'd been expecting.

"I'm confused. I thought my mom only had one older brother?" Haven questioned.

"Apparently not," Faith replied with a defeated shrug. "The journal spells it all out. My mother and her twin sister are the youngest, and by the time our grandmother got pregnant with them, whatever was hiding in that clearing had already begun to corrupt her. The journal mentions a lower-ranking witch who kidnaped the twins and took them to the safety of another coven. My grandparents died when I was a little girl, and I never really knew them, but Fallon told me she never doubted that they were her birth parents. Not until she read the journal. I don't know how long my mom's known the truth about our family, but I do know that she brought us to Canada to try and find the same evil power source that our grandmother found all those years ago. My mother thinks the power inside the clearing is hers by birthright, and she wants it all for herself."

"To what end?" Haven demanded, looking a little pale.

"I don't know," she admitted. "The journal doesn't say what our grandmother's grand plan was or if she ever went looking for the twins after they were taken from her. I know this is a touchy subject, but your mother did the right thing when she killed our grandmother to stop her from siphoning all that evil magic. Now it seems that my mother is trying to follow in her footsteps."

"Do you have the journal? I'd like to see it for myself?" Haven asked with a sorrowful look in her eyes.

Faith felt for her. The level of family betrayal and revelation was intense. "It's at my house, and I need to go back there soon to explain all of this to Fallon. She needs to know what we're up against now that my mother is that, that thing."

"Did the journal happen to mention why the witch who kidnapped Farrow and Fallon left the other two children with our grandmother?"

"No, it didn't. I'm sorry." Faith had wondered the same thing. If the coven member had been so concerned about the twins, why not take all the children to safety?

Running her hands through her hair, Haven huffed. "I don't get why the thing inside the clearing took this long to reemerge. If it was active when our grandmother was alive, then what's it been doing all this time? You've lived here for a few years, and nothing like this has ever happened until now, right?"

Faith cringed as a horrible thought crossed her mind. "Maybe it was waiting for my mother to find it. Maybe it needed someone just as deranged as our grandmother to be its servant."

Sarin chose that moment to knock on the door, and Haven flashed her with a look that screamed oh shit.

"Come in," Faith called out sheepishly.

Sarin pegged her with an accusatory stare as she entered the room.

"Oh, stop with all the theatrics," Haven huffed, "How much did you hear?"

"I heard Faith say *our* grandmother, as in you and her, so what exactly does that mean?"

This wasn't how Faith had planned for this to go down. "I wanted to meet with you last night to explain things. But then the doppelgänger attacked you, and when we got here, well, you know the rest."

Pausing, Faith reminded herself she had no control over Sarin's reaction. The truth would change their relationship for better or worse, and the choice was Sarin's. "My mom's been lying to all for a very long time, and as it turns out, we all share the same DNA."

Sarin's green eyes widened for an instant before she pivoted around and stomped out of the room.

Faith chased after her with Haven close on her heels. "Sarin, wait! Where are you going?"

Dropping her head into her hands, Sarin sat on the couch and began to sob. "It's not fair! All my life, I've wanted to find you, to find a familial connection to my father. Now, my mom will never get to meet Haven or know the truth about you, Faith, and it's all she ever wanted for me."

"I know this is a lot, but it explains our connection and why we've always felt like soul mates," Faith added, hoping to offer her friend—scratch that—her cousin a small amount of comfort. The dramatic shift in their relationship was going to take some getting used to.

"That's true," Sarin admitted between sniffles. "I just miss my mom, and finding out I have more family only magnifies the reality that she's gone."

Haven sat down on one side of Sarin while Faith took the other.

"After I found the journal, I told Fallon I needed to tell you the truth before we confronted Farrow. But now that she's a Dryad, it changes everything. We need to go back to my house and get her and Phoebe. With all of us working together, maybe we can figure out a way to fix this."

Wiping her eyes with the back of her hand, Sarin tried to pull herself together. "I've missed Phoebe so much. I've missed you, too."

"It's time to put an end to all this shit with my mother. But before we go back to my house, I want to see the clearing myself."

"I don't think that's a good idea," Haven stated as she handed Sarin the box of tissues. "Your mother's necklace was there, remember? That means she's lurking around somewhere."

"I can go alone. Last night, she told me it's not me that it wants. If that's true, then maybe I can still reach her." Deep down, Faith hoped that was true.

Haven stood up and began filling a backpack with random supplies. "Fine, but I need to see your necklace before we go. Sarin's bracelet is charmed with a protection spell, and you need one too."

Taking the necklace off, Faith handed the precious heirloom over to Haven.

"And I need to make a second stop at a library before we head to your house."

"For what?" Faith questioned. "Something on your summer reading list?"

"Now she's got jokes," Haven quipped. "A friend told me there might be a book at Raven's Repository that can help us find more information about Dryads, so we're going."

"You've only been in town for a hot second, and you already have a friend who knows about Dryads?" Sarin questioned.

"I didn't say it was a new friend. Did I?" Haven responded with a hint of annoyance in her voice.

Faith felt Haven was hiding something, but she wasn't in a position to question her. "It's completely out of the way, but I know where Raven's is."

Ducking into her room, Haven returned with a pile of clean clothes that she tossed in Faith's direction. "Great. Then get dressed, and let's get going!"

•••

The clearing was just a short hike from the cabin, and as Faith followed behind her two cousins, she marveled at the beauty of the forest. For all her time living in Canada, she'd never gotten out to explore the wilderness. Her mom and aunt had forced her to stay home to keep an eye on her teenage cousins while they'd investigated the forest without them. Today, she felt alive amid the lush canopy of verdant trees, and the fact that the two girls in front of her were of blood relation was an entirely separate revelation.

"You guys! Look at this tree!" she called out as she circled a vast oak. Running her fingers up and down the thick, moss-colored trunk, she swore she could feel magic pulsing inside of it. The sensation was invigorating. The tree was twice as big as the others and had strange, carved markings circling it from root to tree top. The symbols formed beautiful, intricate shapes that she'd never seen before.

Haven grabbed her by the wrist and quickly removed her hand from the tree. "Those are sigils, and you shouldn't touch them."

"What are sigils?" Faith asked with curiosity. The tree had a strange pull over her, and she yearned to touch it again.

"They're magical symbols used for a specific purpose," Sarin cut in. "But we have no idea what these were placed here for."

Taking out her cell phone, she snapped a few pictures of the symbols. "Look here, where the vines are thicker and overlapping. Do you see that shimmer, or is it just me?"

"I see it," Sarin agreed, "and based on what the magic is doing to the land around here, I'm sure it's also affecting the trees."

"We're close now. Keep moving," Haven called out from up ahead.

It was hard for Faith to walk away from the otherworldly tree. Something about the ancient oak called to her, and she didn't understand the protective feeling it invoked inside of her. Thankfully, Sarin was there to gently pull her along. When they reached the clearing, she was surprised by how underwhelming it was. For a magical place with the power to alter animals and turn humans into Dryads, she thought it would pack more of a punch. But all that sat before her was a large, scorched circle of earth.

"Be careful not to step inside...."

Sarin's warning faded to the background when she accidentally placed her foot inside the circle. In the space between one breath and another, she was here and then somewhere else. Gone was the bright morning sunlight. It had been replaced by a grey, monotone landscape that was just as empty as the clearing itself. Her body felt like a live wire as a foreign power vibrated up through the ground, shaking her with the force of an earthquake. The dark and seductive magic called for her to surrender to it, but she held her ground. A red-haired woman who looked a lot like Haven walked toward her through the gray haze with heavy, sorrow-filled eyes.

"I'm sorry about your mother, Faith. I'm sorry I never got the chance to meet her."

She wanted to respond, to tell her it wasn't her fault, but if she opened her mouth, she felt like all the undiluted power running through her would come busting out.

The woman reached out and gently touched her arm. On contact, the monstrous rumble of power inside of her eased enough for her to choke out a few words. "I have to save my mom. Do you know how to reverse the transformation?"

If this woman had a connection to the clearing, then maybe she had information that could help her mother. The woman sighed. The sound was weary and bleak.

"Tell Haven to decipher the sigils. It's the only way."

Before she could ask the woman to elaborate, the world went wonky. Bright daylight hit her eyes like the stab of a knife, and the pain was so intense it made her dry heave. Rolling onto her back, she saw the worried look on Haven's face as she hovered over her. The girl was yelling something, but Faith couldn't hear her over the loud rush of wind in her ears.

"Why am I on the ground? And how did I get over here?" she asked, feeling dazed. She was a few feet outside the clearing.

"Can you hear me?" The words sounded far away, but she knew they belonged to Sarin this time.

"Yes, I can hear you! Your voice is giving me a migraine!"

"Thank god!" Sarin shouted in relief.

"You looked like you were having a seizure, so we pulled you out," Haven said, offering her a bottle of water.

She took the water and used it to rinse out her mouth. The mix of magical residue and bile burning in her throat threatened to make her puke again. "What happened? I was here, and then I was somewhere else, talking to a woman who looked a lot like you, Haven. I've never felt anything like that before."

"The same thing happened to me the first time I came here. The power tried to take me over and control me. Then, when Sarin and I came back, we were transported to the same place you just went. The million-dollar question is - what is that place, and can we get my mom out of there?"

Taking another sip of the water, Faith wiped her mouth off with the hem of her shirt. "Your mother had a message for you. She said you have to decipher the sigils."

"Any chance you know what that means?" Haven asked, looking just as confused as she felt.

"Nope. I was a little too busy having my brain pulled apart to ask her any follow-up questions."

Haven stood up and offered her a hand. "Well, I guess we have more than one book to look for in the library now, so let's get the hell out of here before anything else happens."

Faith couldn't agree more.

CHAPTER 19

Raven's Repository was a tiny gothic masterpiece tucked away at the end of a dreamy tree-lined street, and Haven was in awe of it. Faith and Sarin seemed less than impressed as they drove down the newly paved road that led to the charming building. Its facade boasted two towering turrets and four arched stained-glass windows that twinkled in the mid-day sun. Long before discovering magic and witchcraft, Haven had been a simple girl with a healthy obsession for fantasy books. Now, she barely had time to shower, let alone read, and she wondered if her life would ever resemble that slow-paced average human existence ever gain. And speaking of showers, they all needed to take care of that little ritual when they got back to Faith's house because it was getting ripe up in this car. Parking in the empty lot, Haven noticed the *Closed* sign hanging in the stained-glass window on the side of the front door. Just that morning, another news report had gone out about strange electrical surges going on around Huntsville. The library was a good fifteen miles from town, so maybe the owners were just being cautious. Or maybe they weren't open on Mondays. She hadn't bothered to Google their hours of operation before driving over. Exiting the car, she felt on edge, but that was par for the course these days.

"Do you think they have cameras?" Sarin asked as she peered inside the front window.

"Even if they do. We'll be in and out before the police have time to get here. This place is in the middle of nowhere," Haven said as she placed her hand over the doorknob. "Now do me a favor and shush while I cast a little breaking and entering spell."

Sarin shot her some side-eye over the comment, which made her smile. The girl had a lot of spark when she wasn't a broken, crying mess. That fire would serve her well when the shit with Farrow hit the fan.

After repeating the words to the spell three times, the door to the library swung open with a loud creak. Crossing the threshold, her nose was assaulted by the smell of aged parchment and leather. The familiar scent felt like coming home. Sunlight danced off the dusty wooden floors as it filtered through the windows, and the occasional creak of a floorboard only added to the library's ghostly atmosphere. Lucifer had been spot on when he'd said no one would notice an ancient-looking book hidden here. The library had dozens of towering bookshelves that housed hundreds of books, including an entire section of books that had nothing but mysterious symbols on their covers. It was overwhelming, and Haven had no idea where to start. She went left while motioning for Faith and Sarin to search on the right.

Sarin pulled a book from a random shelf and coughed when a plume of dust washed over her. "What exactly are we looking for?"

"Anything that feels different. The book I'm looking for should give off a big amount of magical energy."

She heard Faith snort and knew what was coming next. "So, this mysterious friend of yours knows all about Dryads and magical books?"

"Yeah, Haven, care to elaborate?" Sarin added as she dusted off her shirt.

She didn't feel like indulging them at the moment. They had a job to do. "I don't. But maybe we can have a little cousin gossip sesh later if you find what we're looking for."

Running her finger down the spine of an old, worn book, Haven wished she could be an ordinary girl again, just for a day. An entire day where she could sit and let a book transport her to another place. She was a horror lover at heart, but now that she knew nightmarish things with claws and teeth really did exist out in the world, it completely killed the vibe. Now, if she ever got back into reading, it would be romance or cottage-core all the way. After searching aisle after aisle and coming up empty, she finally spotted an ornate-looking door near the library's back office. The wood panel in the center of the door was engraved with an intricate depiction of Raven's Raven in flight, which was fitting for the library's name. Pushing it open, she was immediately drawn to a shelf in the middle row. True to Lucifer's promise, a large leather-bound book with filigreed gold edges sat on full display. The book looked like it belonged to the Earth, with swirling vines of gold and green adorning the cover. It had no title, but the power emanating from it proved it was the one she was looking for. A loud bang rang out from outside the door, and she jumped at the sound.

"Sorry!" Sarin yelled. "Did I ever mention that I'm clumsy?"

"Shit, Sarin, you scared me! And why are you yelling when we're supposed to be incognito?" Haven asked as she placed the book inside her messenger bag.

Sarin looked around and shrugged. "There's no one else in here, so I don't see the need to whisper. I found a few books mentioning sigils, so I grabbed them too."

"Great. Put them in here," Haven urged as she opened the top of her.

The jingling of keys and the creak of the front door had them running for cover behind the nearest bookshelf. Holding her breath, Haven motioned for the other girls to stay still.

"I don't want any trouble. Just take whatever you came for and get out," the familiar male voice called out.

This couldn't be happening. Not right now. Standing to face a person she never expected to see in Canada, Haven silently cursed the universe for continuing to fuck with her.

"What are you doing?" Faith whispered as she pulled on Haven's shirt to try and keep her hidden.

"It's fine, guys. I know him," Haven announced as she took in the sight of her ex-boyfriend, who was staring over at her like he'd seen just a ghost.

The feeling was mutual.

"Hey, Adam. Long time no see."

As Sarin and Faith stood up beside her, she tried to keep her composure calm, but inside, she was officially freaking out. There was no way this was just a conscience, no way that he'd accidentally stumbled upon her here. The most pressing question was, who had arranged this meeting, and why? When she jumped through the portal and left her dad without a word, she'd also left Adam. She owed him an apology and had been planning on giving him one, but this impromptu meeting was a shock.

Crossing his thick arms over his chest, he shot her a look filled with disdain. "Stealing now? That's a new low, even for you."

She felt her cheeks heat up as anger colored her expression. "Thanks, I missed you too. By the way, what the fuck are you doing in Canada?"

"Isn't it obvious?" he spat. "I came here to find you after our friends told me where you were. But you're a hard one to pin down, with all the lies and whatnot."

She knew he meant witchcraft and magic instead of lies and whatnot, but to his credit, he was attempting to keep her secret. "You can speak freely; they know what I am. They're my cousins."

His mouth fell open at her admission. "Cousins?"

"Yes. Apparently, my mother had some very tight-lipped secrets of her own."

"Well, hi. I'm Adam, and this is super uncomfortable, but um, it's nice to meet you?"

It was typical of him to try and be gracious, even under these strange circumstances, and his kind heart made her feel like an even bigger asshole.

"Yeah, we got your name," Sarin said in a suspicious voice, "But why are you here? In this particular bookstore? If you couldn't find her before, then how is it that you just happened to be here today."

She didn't love Sarin's tone, but the girl was spot on. This entire thing seemed orchestrated.

"I wasn't sure how long I'd be in town, so I thought it would be smart to get a part-time job while I was here. This job popped up on Indeed yesterday, so I applied. The owner called me a few hours later and asked me to come in for a test shift, which went well, so she asked me to come back today to do inventory."

Faith opened her mouth to say something, but Haven shushed her.

"Do you mind waiting in the car? Adam and I need a moment."

Sarin shot her a questioning look as she grabbed the bag of stolen books and ushered Faith out the front door. Once they were alone, she noticed how much older Adam looked. He had worry lines etched into his handsome face, and she felt a ping of regret over how she'd left things. They'd drifted apart long before she'd chosen to come to Canada, and she'd been too afraid to let him go until now. The guy had been through his own version of hell after murdering a girl at their old high school while he'd been possessed, and since then, he preferred to steer clear of anything magic or supernatural.

"I agree with my cousin, Adam. You're not here by chance. I think a much bigger force brought you here, and I don't understand why, so I suggest you go back home. Right now." His parents owned a plant store back in Colorado, and when his familiar scent of lavender and sage wafted over to her, she swallowed down the rising lump in her chest.

Cursing, Adam leaned back against one of the bookshelves. "I hate all this magic shit, you know that. I honestly thought I came here of my free will to find you and make sure you were okay. The idea that something else might have manipulated my choices doesn't sit well with me."

"I don't know if I'm okay, but I'm here, and all that magic shit is a package deal with me. I'm sorry I didn't call you after I left. I'm sorry for a lot of things, but I won't apologize for what I am, and no matter how much you love me, this witch shit will be a deal breaker for you at some point. I intended to come back to tell you all of this in person, but it looks like someone, or something brought you to me instead."

Warm memories of their first date at the dreamy bookstore back in Colorado threatened to bring on her tears, especially as he stared at her with a look of longing. "I can't be what you want, Adam. The fact that you're here right now proves that. You want a normal life, and my life is the complete opposite. I'm not willing to give up my magic, and you shouldn't have to be involved in a world you want no part in. So go home, Adam. I loved our time together, but it's over."

She watched as a kaleidoscope of emotions passed across his face. "Aside from worrying about you, I've been relatively happy. Ever since you ran off to do your little whatever in Florida, things back home have been pretty normal, and honestly, I hope they stay that way. And to your point, I do love you, and I don't think outside forces are the only reason I came here."

She was skeptical. "You flew all the way to Canada to look for me, stumbled upon a job without a work permit or visa, and then found me at your place of employment the very next day. You don't find that weird? Think back over the last few weeks, Adam. Did you really want to come here, or did something push you? No matter how much you love me, this doesn't feel like you. You're a rule-follower at heart, not a *jump-on-a-plane and fly-by-the-seat-of-your-pants* guy."

"None of that matters. I'm here now, and we're having a conversation that needed to be had, right?"

He was right about the conversation part, but whatever or whoever had brought him here didn't do it out of the kindness of their heart, and she would never forgive herself if he got hurt because of her. "I'm dealing with some next-level dangerous magic right now, and the fact that you just swooped in and found me is downright scary. I don't want anything bad to happen to you, so I need you to leave right now and head straight to the airport. Give me your hand."

He turned a little pale at her request. "No. I'll go, but I'm not letting you use magic on me. I'll be fine!"

She understood his hesitation, but this was for his protection. "I can't let you go without ensuring you make it home safely."

Taking a step away from her, his expression turned bitter. "That's exactly why I won't let you cast a spell on me. I won't be magically manipulated on purpose. Especially if someone or something already used magic to get me here."

She knew him well enough to know that once his mind was made up, there was no changing it. A picture of Lucifer's face flashed inside her mind, and she wanted to scream. Of course, he had something to do with this. He was the one who'd sent her to the library, so it made sense that he had something to do with Adam's presence. That fact gave her a small amount of relief but also filled her with rage. No one had the right to meddle in her personal life. Especially not Lucifer. She still had no idea what he truly wanted from her, but if he was the one behind this, it was less terrifying. If the magic from the clearing or Farrow were to blame, then that would be much, much worse.

"Fine! But promise you'll call me when you get to the airport, and again when you land. I can't go with you, and it's not safe for you to stay in town."

"Just like you called me?" The accusation was cruel but true.

"Look, I get it. I was a major ass-hat to you, and I'm sorry. But I need to know you're safe. So, please?"

He still looked royally pissed but nodded in acceptance. "Why did you break in here? Was it just to steal some old books?"

"For some magical shit, you just said you want nothing to do with."

"Fair enough," he declared as he motioned for her to exit the bookstore.

Following her outside, he locked things up before unexpectedly pulling her in for a hug. She was stiff at first, but eventually, she loosened up and hugged him back. For all she knew, this could be the last time they ever saw each other.

"What am I going to tell the owners?" he asked as they ended their embrace.

"I'm sure you'll figure something out." If he wanted to keep magic out of the equation, he'd have to deal with all the real-life consequences.

As she headed to the car, under the watchful eyes of her cousins, she called back. "Keep your promise, Adam, and thank you for coming to check on me, even if it wasn't all you're doing."

He was the last piece of the puzzle that represented her old life, and as he waved goodbye, she had a profound feeling that everything else was about to change.

CHAPTER 20

Faith wasn't sure what the hell had just gone down, but she couldn't deny the uncomfortable feeling in her gut over Haven's unplanned reunion.

As Haven slid into the driver's seat, she rested her head against the headrest and let out a loud sigh. "Don't say a word, not one word!"

Faith couldn't help herself. "Some mysterious friend of yours leads us to the middle of nowhere to find a mythical book, and then, your hottie ex-boyfriend shows up in the same place, and we're not supposed to ask any questions. As if!"

"Adam and I went to high school together, and later, we became more than friends. He was my first everything, and I left him without an explanation. He followed me here, and we said what we needed to say. Now it's over," Haven offered as she white-knuckled the steering wheel.

Sarin whistled low from her position in the front seat. "You must have really given him the goods if he followed you all the way from Colorado."

"Oh, shut up, Sarin," Haven replied with a hint of a smile. "His presence here wasn't just by chance. Adam's a sweet guy, but he didn't come here, all knight in shining armor style."

Her palms began to sweat as Haven pulled the car onto Highway 60. This thing with Adam was an unexpected complication. "Why would someone send him here?"

"To distract me or throw me off my game. Honestly, I have no idea."

It was alarming that someone or something was trying to mess with Haven. She was the strongest of them all, and they needed her to be in it to win it. But maybe that's why she was being targeted. Take her out, and they all fell.

"What did you say to him?" Sarin asked.

"I told him to get on the next flight back to Colorado. I just hope he listens. Worrying about him is a distraction I can't afford right now."

Faith couldn't agree more. It was going to be hard enough to explain the whole Dryad situation to her aunt, Fallon. God knew that woman had enough on her plate right now.

The glint of gold filigree caught Faith's eye from inside the messenger bag. "Haven, do you mind if I skim through the book?"

"Sure, but be careful. I was told it has sentience," Haven warned as she whipped the car around a sharp turn.

The momentum sent the bag tumbling to the floor, and all the books spilled out.

"What does that cryptic shit mean? Faith questioned as she leaned over to pick up the book she wanted.

"I don't know! That's why I said be careful," Haven declared with a hint of annoyance in her voice.

"What's the worst that could happen?" Sarin joked.

Faith pegged Sarin with a harsh stare as a million horrible thoughts came to mind. "Oh, I don't know, maybe we accidentally create another evil monster and unleash it into the world?"

Sarin's smile faded. "Yeah, let's not do that again!"

Placing the ancient-looking book in her lap, she felt a sense of calm wash over her as she ran her hand over the cover. The combination of gold, green, and filigree was a feast for the eyes, but the book itself had no title. Opening it up, she was surprised to find that it was all about Greek Mythology. Thumbing through the worn pages, it didn't take long for her to find the section on Dryad's. The book listed the different types of Dryads under separate categories, but each section began with a basic description, and as she read on, her skin broke out in a cold sweat as the chilling realization of what had been done to her mother hit home. According to the book, Dryads were considered minor goddesses that lived among the trees. They could take on the form of young, beautiful men or women and were often described as vengeful creatures created by the forest to protect it. The Greeks would make offerings to the Dryads at harvest time, and in turn, the Dryads cultivated their lands for them for a price. The Greeks also believed the Dryads had no regard for human life or human feelings and feared their vengeance. Faith blanched at that notion. When her mother confronted her at the cabin, her eyes seemed vacant and devoid of all emotion.

The book went on to highlight the five different types of Dryads, which all had different characteristics. The Meliai were said to be tied to ash trees, while The Oreiades preferred mountain conifers. The Hamadryades liked oak, especially the kind that grew around riverbeds, and their life force was said to be tied to the tree they resided in. Then there were The Maliades, who took care of the fruit trees, and, lastly, The Daphne, who were associated with laurel trees and thought to be the originators of the Dryad line. Based on what the book described and what Farrow had told her in person, it was becoming apparent that the dark magic inside the clearing had turned Farrow into a Dryad so she could be its harbinger—or maybe its protector. But to what end? And could the transformation be reversed?

Haven took another turn at breakneck speed. If her cousin kept this up, Faith was going to lose her breakfast all over the backseat. Repositioning the book, a folded-up piece of paper fell out and landed on her lap. Unfolding the paper, she was impressed by the impeccable handwriting.

I hope you found what you needed. This particular story isn't in the book, but I thought it might be helpful.

Daphne and Apollo

Daphne was a dryad who spent most of her time by the river. The daughter of a river God, she never ventured too far from the life-giving waters. One day, the great God Apollo insulted the God Eros, and as punishment, Eros shot Apollo with a golden arrow that made him fall in love with Daphne. To add insult to injury, Eros shot a second arrow into Daphne to ensure she could never reciprocate Apollo's feelings. You see, Eros was the God of love, but in his rage, he vowed never to let Apollo feel the joy that love could bring. Apollo pursued Daphne relentlessly, but she always ran from him. Then, one day, Daphne left the forest and ran to the river to beg her father, Peneus, for help, which he gladly offered, and when Apollo finally caught up to Daphne and touched her skin, she changed. Her skin turned to bark, and her limbs turned into branches. Apollo watched in horror as his love was transformed into a laurel tree. Peneus thought he was saving Daphne from harm by turning her into a mighty tree, and Apollo, in his grief, swore to watch over her for all time, even imbuing her with immortality so her tree would always remain.

Faith gaped at the private note that was clearly meant for Haven's eyes. The story of Daphne and Apollo made her feel sick to her stomach. But what did it mean? Especially the last line about the tree and its roots. Once they got back to her house and Haven had a chance to read the note, they had a lot to discuss. Staring out the window, Faith took in the view of the Muskoka River as they drove through the familiar streets of downtown Huntsville. The majestic waterway that ran through town sat frozen. Its once raging waves put on pause as if Bob Ross had painted the scene on a blank canvas. Sarin's small gasp of shock was the only indication that either of her cousins had noticed the anomaly, and they were either too freaked out to speak up or making the conscious choice to ignore the cataclysmic sight. Faith was choosing to be ignorant until they got a handle on the Dryad situation. Re-folding the piece of paper, she couldn't help but notice the strong smell of sulfur that wafted from the parchment.

The abrupt stop of the car brought her thoughts back to the present, and as she handed the note to Haven, she couldn't help but ask, "So, who exactly is L?"

CHAPTER 21

Sarin looked back and forth between her cousins as Haven parked the car on the street in front of Faith's house. The tension in the air was palpable as she waited for Haven to answer Faith's question.

"I already told Sarin there are some things about my past that I'm not ready to share, and this is one of them. I'm not trying to be rude, but I barely know either of you, and my story is a lot to take in. When this mess with Farrow is all said and done, and we have more time to get to know each other, I swear I'll explain it all."

She'd heard this line before and accepted it for the time being, but she wasn't so sure Faith was willing to do the same, especially since Farrow had kept the truth from her for so long. But to her surprise, Faith didn't put up a fight.

"I don't like secrets, but you're right. We need to focus on helping my mom, and as long as whatever you're hiding doesn't hinder that, I can wait for the truth."

Sarin could have sworn Haven's bright green eyes glossed over for an instant before the girl jumped out of the car. It took a second for her to muster up the courage to do the same. The last time she'd come to this house had been to confront Farrow, and then her life had taken a detour. Phoebe came running out of the house, and her heart did a flip-flop as the teen headed straight for her.

"I thought I'd never see you again," Phoebe cried as she tackled her with a big bear hug.

Wrapping her arms around her friend, she was grateful to be reunited with her, but Selene's absence was palpable. The twins had been inseparable when Selene was alive, and in that moment, she wished the doppelgänger was still alive so she could kill it all over again. "You sneaky little witch! You were my undercover cousin this entire time." Phoebe said as she pulled back. The look of longing and sadness in her young eyes was palpable.

"And you..." Phoebe gestured to Haven. "Wow! You look so much like Sarin. It's really quite off-putting."

"It's nice to meet you too, cousin," Haven said with a grin.

"I appreciate a little sarcasm in my family members," Phoebe joked. "Now, let's get inside, mom's waiting."

Phoebe ushered them into the kitchen, where Fallon was waiting at the breakfast nook with a cup of coffee in hand. Faith and Phoebe sat down at the table, but Sarin lingered in the doorway. Being surrounded by all of them felt intimate, and she wasn't ready to go all in with the family thing just yet. Haven seemed to mirror her sentiment as she leaned back against the sink. The familiar scent of Faith's home hit her like a punch to the gut. Fallon wasn't a threat, but the last time she'd been here, things between them hadn't ended on good terms. Fallon stared at her with a deep look of regret in her stormy grey eyes. She wanted to say something, to apologize for her part in what had happened to Selene, but when she opened her mouth, nothing came out.

"It's okay, Sarin. I know you never meant to hurt Selene, and I won't let my sister hurt you, either," Fallon announced as if she were reading her mind.

Sarin wanted to believe her, but trust took time to build.

"Faith told me she filled you in on all the family drama, so you already know I'm your aunt." Motioning to Haven, Fallon added, "And yours too. I know it's shocking, but everything makes sense now."

"I thought you were going to wait for me to come home before you told Phoebe?" Faith asked as she took a seat next to Fallon.

"Have you met Phoebe?" Fallon asked with an eye roll. "When you didn't come home last night, she went ballistic, and I was forced to explain it all. She's a tenacious little tornado, that one."

"Hello? I'm right here!" Phoebe chimed in.

She smiled at their banter. It felt like a little piece of normalcy amidst the chaos. Phoebe was willful on a good day and an annoying people-pusher on an average one.

"Auntie?" Faith nudged. "There's something else that we need to talk about."

Faith tensed up as she prepared to break the news about Farrow's current state of being, and Sarin felt horrible for all of them. Fallon had planned to confront her twin sister, not some monstrous creature.

When Faith sat there, looking like a deer in headlights, she took over for her. "Something happened to Farrow out in those woods. Something changed her."

"Changed her how?" Fallon demanded.

She looked at Faith to see if she wanted to take over, but her friend was staring at the table, fidgeting with her ring. It was something she did whenever she felt uncomfortable.

"I don't know how to sugarcoat this," Sarin admitted. "So, I'm just going to say it. Some magical force inside those woods turned her into a Dryad. Do you know what that is?"

Fallon's coffee cup slipped from her hand, and to Sarin's amazement, she used her power to freeze the scalding liquid mid-air before it could stain her linen pants. The coffee droplets swirled around in the air until Fallon righted her cup and commanded the liquid to flow back into its waiting container. The open display of magic was impressive. Fallon and Farrow had never actively practiced in front of any of them before.

"Don't look so surprised, Sarin. I have no reason to withhold my magic in this house anymore. How do you know she's a Dryad? Did any of you see her for yourselves?"

Faith looked away at Fallon's question. "She attacked me outside of Haven's cabin."

"Did she hurt you? Any of you?" Fallon asked as she took Faith by the hand.

She couldn't begin to imagine what Faith was going through. Her own mother was gone, and that was hard enough to process, but Faith's mother was still here, still tangible, just an entirely different version of herself. A terrifying, bloodthirsty version that was capable of anything. Faith had already lost the mother she thought she had, and now, if they couldn't fix Farrow, she might lose her all over again to death. It was heartbreaking to think you could lose someone twice.

Shaking her platinum blonde head, Faith finally spoke up. "I'm fine. But she wants to keep us far away from that clearing. Whatever's hiding out there is what did this to her."

"I planned on talking some sense into my sister, but it seems that ship has sailed," Fallon commented in a defeated voice.

"Do you know anything about sigils?" Sarin asked as she pulled the stolen books out of Haven's messenger bag.

Placing the books in front of Fallon, she hoped the older witch might have some insight. "We found a collection of them carved into a tree in the forest, and then Faith had a vision or some kind of contact with Haven's mother when she stepped into the clearing. Haven's mother told her we have to decipher the sigils, but we don't know what that means."

"How did Haven's mother contact you? The journal claims our other siblings were killed, so was she alive, or was it some kind of spirit?"

Faith filled her in on her experience, and then Sarin added, "The first time I went to the clearing with Haven, the same thing happened to us. I'm not sure if that desolate place is real or if the magic in the clearing is messing with us."

A look of frustration spread across Fallon's face as she thumbed through one of the books. "This is bad. If the magic in the clearing has her trapped somewhere, I'm not sure we can pull her out. If she's dead, and this is all a trick, what's its motivation?"

"You worry about your sister and leave my mother to me," Haven's voice was firm, almost commanding, as she addressed Fallon from the other side of the kitchen.

Fallon's eyes narrowed at Haven's harsh words, but to her credit, she didn't react.

"To answer your question, Sarin, sigils have been around as long as Witchcraft itself. They're normally used to summon something or cast something out."

Sarin's eyes went wide as a light bulb went off. "So, you're saying we could potentially use them to cast out whatever's inside the clearing?"

"The Void," Fallon stated.

"The what?" Faith and Haven asked in unison.

"It's called The Void, or at least that's what Farrow used to call it. We came to Canada because my sister was looking for a legendary well of magic, one of only a few left in the world. Farrow told me she wanted to find it but failed to mention that our family had been attempting to siphon its power for years. Farrow claimed it was a sacred place that needed our protection, and it was our coven's duty to care for it. The Void can be contained but not destroyed. I need you girls to take me there so I can better assess the situation."

"And what are your plans for Farrow now?" Sarin asked in a shaky voice. "She still wants me dead, and from what we saw, she's not exactly human anymore."

Fallon's features remained stoic as she took a sip of her coffee. "Leave my sister to me, like Haven suggested."

Haven's posture went rigid, and Sarin could tell her cousin was getting uncomfortable. The tension in the room was palpable, so she took the opportunity to remove them from the situation.

Picking up one of the books, she motioned for Haven to follow her. "Haven, can I talk to you in private?"

"Why are you leaving?" Faith asked as Sarin attempted to sneak out of the kitchen.

"I think the three of you could use some time to talk as a family. I'm going to take Haven to your room and read up on these sigils."

"But you're our family now, too," Phoebe said softly.

Her heart warmed at Phoebe's kind words, but the reality of their family situation was a lot to grasp, and she needed time to process—time she didn't have right now.

Shrugging, she said, "You know what I mean. Haven and I are going to go camp out in Faith's room and read. We won't be far."

Sarin could sense their disappointment, but being in a room with all of them was overstimulating, especially when her mother's death was still so fresh in her heart.

"You want to tell me what all that was about?" Haven asked as Sarin all but dragged her down the hallway to Faith's bedroom.

"You looked like you needed a breather. I know I did."

"Good point," Haven said as she followed her into Faith's room.

Curling up on Faith's bed, Sarin remembered all the nights she'd spent in this room, talking to her best friend into the early morning hours. Now, the room felt foreign, just like everything else in her life.

"I know they're both excited about this new family connection, but I need a little space. Three days ago, my mom was alive, Faith was just a friend, and I was on the track to finishing my second year of nursing school. Now, my mom is dead, a mythical Dryad is after me, and I have a bunch of cousins who I never knew existed. It's pure insanity, and my brain feels like it might explode. You can't tell me you're okay with all of this? I saw your face turn bright red when you were talking to Fallon."

Haven laid back against the pillows and rested her head next to Sarin's. "I'm not okay with it, but the supernatural world isn't new to me, and I've had more time to come to terms with certain things. Meeting you wasn't something I expected, but I'm happy it happened, and I'm willing to give those girls a chance because they're our family. I mean, I didn't know you a few days ago and look how well that's going." Haven said jokingly as she nudged her on the arm. "But I get it. The whole Adam thing is really upsetting me, and right now, I'd rather investigate how he got here than cozy up with our long-lost relatives. I'm not sure why I let Fallon get under my skin but thank you for giving me an out."

She didn't want to push, but she was desperate to know more about Adam and the mysterious L from the letter.

True to form, Haven figured out what she was thinking before she spoke, "You're projecting, and you need to work on shielding your thoughts. I'm still a novice when it comes to mind reading, but your thoughts are screaming at me. And fine, if it will shut you up, I'll spill the tea. Like I mentioned earlier, Adam was my first real boyfriend, and I lost my virginity to him. He went through a lot of bad shit when we were in high school and now has a strict no-magic policy. So, you see the problem. Anyway, I left him behind when I came here and never gave him a proper goodbye until today."

"How are you feeling about that?" Sarin asked as she rolled onto her side to give Haven her undivided attention.

"A little sad but mostly relieved. I love Adam, but I refuse to deny the magical part of myself for any relationship, and he deserves a normal life if that's what he wants."

A ping of sadness spread inside Sarin's chest. "I know what you mean. Alex and I broke things off long before I ever considered telling him my secret. But if he knew what I really was and rejected that part of me, I would have been devastated. I can't believe he's gone now, too."

As she pictured Alex's handsome face, fresh tears welled in her eyes.

"Finding someone who can handle that truth about us is going to be a challenge, but my parents found each other, and so did yours." Grinning, Haven added, "I haven't met any boy witches yet, but they have to exist, right? I mean, that would be the easiest solution."

"If they don't, I'm totally down for a lady witch," Sarin admitted.

Haven's warm smile helped ease the somber mood. "Well, cheers to you. I'll be royally screwed if girls are all we have to work with. And since we're being honest with each other, I'm not ready to talk about L just yet, but there is something you can help me with that involves him."

Her interest was piqued. "Like what?"

"I need to talk to him, but I have to cast an astral projection spell to do it. Can you keep our aunt and cousins occupied for an hour or so?"

"If I do this, will you promise to tell me the truth about him when you get back?"

"Yes. As soon as it's feasible," Haven agreed.

"I feel like that's a very vague time frame, but since you helped me more times than I can count, I'll do this for you," Sarin offered as she scooted off the bed.

"There's one more thing. Can you distract them by making them read through some of those books while I'm gone? After all, you did tell them we were coming in here to do research, and we need to understand how those sigils might help us."

"Two favors? You're going to owe me big time!"

Leaving Haven alone in Faith's room, she felt like a ball of conflicting emotions as she padded down the hallway toward her newfound family—a family she'd wished for but was now scared to be a part of. Fallon had never been kind to her, and she wasn't sure she could put all her anger aside and embrace her aunt with open arms. But when she walked into the kitchen and saw Faith's bright, welcoming smile, she reminded herself that maybe she could. Maybe there was still a little room left in her broken heart for these three women who had all been hurt and lied to, just like her.

CHAPTER 22

Haven tried to calm her racing thoughts enough to astral project, but her brain shot her the middle finger. The conversation with Fallon had only magnified her concerns over her own mother. If she was still alive and trapped, Haven hoped she could bring her back, but if her image was just a cruel trick created by The Void, then it was back to square one. Turning her focus back on the task at hand, she paused. What if she ended up in a worse place this time? Closing her eyes, she tried to visualize every inch of Lucifer's private chamber before casting the astral projection spell. There was no way to ensure her magic didn't rebuke her again, but having a clear target felt like a good start. Letting her magic whisk her soul away, she let out a shaky breath when she reformed inside the familiar lounge that belonged to the king of Hell. The lavish room was empty, and she wasn't in the mood to sit around and wait for Lucifer to grace her with his prescience—not when all she wanted to do was scream at him for the whole Adam debacle. How dare he not be here! Taking the rare opportunity to snoop, she flittered around the room, opening drawers and searching through random buffet cabinets, thankful when nothing creepy jumped out at her. There were no shrunken heads or jars of hearts to be seen.

A rhythmic thumping noise caught her ear from behind her. Turning toward the source of the sound, she traced the noise to the floor-length mirror that sat behind the couch. Against her better judgment, she pressed her ear against the mirror, and when she did, a loud moan reverberated from within. Reaching out, she gently stroked the surface of the glass. Her image blurred before revealing a very graphic and very unwanted carnal display on the other side of the glass. Lucifer was standing at the end of a massive four-poster bed, thrusting himself in and out of a humanish-looking woman who was moaning in ecstasy. Embarrassed and disgusted by the sight of him with another woman, she ripped her hand back from the mirror. Staring at her reflection once more, she backed away from the mirror as a fresh flood of rage washed over her. In her haste to retreat from the unwanted peep show, she bumped into the buffet cabinet and knocked over a few of Lucifer's cocktail glasses. As they shattered on the floor, Lucifer stepped out from inside the mirror. He was glistening with sweat and completely naked. Placing her arm in front of her face, she tried to shield her eyes. She didn't need or want to see the image of him full frontal. Okay, who was she kidding? She totally wanted to see it, but not after she'd just witnessed him having sex with another woman. Clenching her fists, she felt like punching him or, better yet, murdering the woman in his bed. Was she jealous? Because that's exactly what the insidious feeling rising in her throat felt like.

Anger colored his features as he assessed his private chamber, but his eyes softened when they landed on her. "Dammit, Haven. Let me put on some pants!"

Snapping his fingers, he uttered, "You can look now."

He'd materialized a pair of faded black jeans over the lower part of his body, but his chest was still bare. Speaking toward the mirror in a stream of hurried whispers, he ordered the harlot to get out of bed. Staring over at him, her breath caught at the glorious sight of him all shirtless and disheveled. Reminding herself why she'd come here in the first place, she let her resentful feelings take the place of any sexual thoughts she might be having about him.

"What are you doing here?" he demanded. "This isn't a good time!"

"Obviously," she said with an eye roll. Nice little trick with the mirror, by the way."

"Your captives can't kill you if they don't know where you sleep."

He said it all casually, like waiting for people to kill him was an everyday thing. She supposed it was when you were the ruler of the place that housed all the world's evil.

"That theory only works if the girl you're banging never gets mad at you because obviously she knows where you sleep."

"Maybe that's just where I have sex," he quipped.

He was infuriating. "You know what? I didn't come here for this!"

The sexy smile he flashed her made her blood boil. "Then why did you come, little witch?"

"I came to tell you to stay out of my fucking business!"

Lucifer smiled again, but this time, the gesture was anything but pleasant. "A few days ago, you very much wanted me to be all up in your business when you needed my help."

"I asked for your help with the Dryad situation. I didn't give you permission to manipulate the people in my personal life. Does the name Adam ring a bell? He's smart, I'll give him that, but he doesn't have any magic of his own, and there's no way he could have found me on his own. What did you do?"

Lucifer put his hands up in surrender. "Fine, fine! You caught me red-handed. But you and the young human needed closure. I helped, so you should be thanking me."

His level of entitlement was exasperating. "Why do you care about my love life? Maybe I'm missing something, but when I got here, you were busy fucking someone else! If you want me, just say it! Don't go around meddling with the people I care about to get my attention!"

The rims around Lucifer's ebony eyes blazed red. "You made it very clear the last time I touched you that you were appalled by the real me, so why would I think you would let me touch you again?"

He was right, but she was still angry. He had no right to mind fuck the people in her life in order to get what he wanted. Whatever that might be, "Just tell me what you want with me, and let's be done with this. Adam's innocent, and you went too far."

"Maybe? But to embrace what's to come, you need to let go of the past. The boy made his way back home. He's safe and sound; I made sure of it."

"I didn't ask you if he was fine. I said you were out of line for involving him in the first place." She didn't owe him any thanks when he was the cause of the problem.

Stomping over to the bar, Lucifer filled his glass with the amber-colored liquid he liked to drink. "If you want the truth, here it is. I didn't mean for our connection to happen. When you tapped into my power through The Devil's Chair, it created a bond between us that I've never had with anyone else. I can read you through the bond, and you kept hesitating when it came to the boy, so I created a situation to help you say goodbye. At first,

I wanted to try and use our connection to my advantage, but then I found myself thinking about you and..."

"And, what?" Haven snapped.

"I realized I have feelings for you," he declared with a hint of vulnerability in his voice.

Her stomach clenched in response to his admission. She couldn't deny that she had feelings for him, too, not after today, but even if she wanted to entertain them, they still had a huge logistical problem. "What does that mean for someone like you? Are you even capable of love? And how exactly would that work when you're trapped in Hell, and my life is up there?"

"Exactly!" he shot back. "That's exactly why I didn't want to tell you. It's an impossible situation. You asked for honesty, so here it is. You played an integral part in releasing Samuel from his sentence in Purgatory, and together, we helped God escape from Heaven. I've been stuck here since the beginning, resigned to my fate. I'm tired, Haven, so very tired of ruling this place, and that's what I want from you. I want you to help me leave Hell."

And there it was, she thought, the real reason he wanted her. His big speech about feelings for her was nothing but bullshit, and she cursed herself for craving it. "Even if I wanted that for you, I'm not sure I can make it happen. It took all my power, your power, and a human soul to transfer Samuel's reprieve to God."

"This time, all you have to do is perform a spell for me."

Nothing was that simple. "Just one little innocent spell for the ruler of Hell? And let me guess, it requires another soul, a gallon of innocent blood, or some other fucked up ingredient I'm not willing to provide."

"All I need is for you to cast the spell from inside Hell," he said with a smile that made her wish his feelings for her were genuine.

"If it's that easy, let's do it right now," she offered, desperate to end this pointless song and dance with him.

Putting his glass down, Lucifer stalked over to her. The sweat on his chest glistened in the firelight, and she felt her throat tighten as she took in the sheer size of him. Placing his hand under her chin, he tipped her face up to meet his. "If the spell works and I walk free, will you let me touch you then?"

Her body screamed a resounding yes, but the sickening image of him banging that other woman shook her out of it.

Stepping back, she offered him a cold smile. "I think you already have someone for that."

Disappointment colored his features as he dropped his hand. "She's of no importance to me. I have needs like everyone else, but if I had the choice, you would be in my bed right now."

Her body shivered under the sexy weight of his words, but she stood her ground. "I hope the spell can give you what you want, but it doesn't include me."

His dark eyes lit with a hint of challenge. "I've grown very patient in my old age, and I'm confident you'll come around to my affections in time."

She didn't trust herself to be alone with him when he was looking at her like that. "I have a raging Dryad and a Void of evil magic to deal with, so can we skip the sexy banter and just get to the point?"

"You're quite cute when you're flustered," he pointed out.

She was done playing games. Grabbing onto the proverbial string that led back to her body, she called on her magic to send her home. "That's it. I'm leaving. You can figure this shit out on your own."

"Wait!" he called after her.

"Give me one good reason why I should?"

"Because I helped you save the fucking world, and now I'm trying to help you stop that raging Dryad, as you called her."

He was annoyingly right, yet again. "You have five minutes to convince me."

"Challenge accepted," he offered as he walked back over to the bar. "I need you to cast a spell to help me find the Antichrist."

She wasn't sure she'd heard him correctly. "Come again?"

"Did I stutter?" he mocked as he refilled his glass. "If I want to leave this place, then someone else must rule it. The spell will tell us if the Antichrist is already in existence or when it will come to pass."

One of her best friends had prophesied the return of the Antichrist, and this new revelation sent a shiver down her spine." If everything in this place is evil, why can't you just leave it alone and let it destroy itself?"

He ran a hand through his wavy black hair. "While I agree with you, I can't physically leave this place unless my seat is replaced, and I have a sinking feeling that Hell won't accept just anyone. Rules of the Realms and all. The most suitable replacement would be a powerful being like the Antichrist."

If his statement about The Realms was true, then someone had been forced to take over Purgatory since Samuel's departure. That idea scared her, but the God situation was much worse. If He didn't return to Heaven, then someone else would have a claim on that Realm as well. Pinching the bridge of her nose, she tried to ease the oncoming migraine. "What if the Antichrist isn't due for centuries?"

"Then, I wait. Like I always have."

"I'll be dead by the time that happens," she regretted the words as soon as they left her lips. She didn't know what she was saying anymore.

"If I don't get to walk free in your lifetime, you're always welcome to visit me here, my little witch."

Studying his handsome face, she tried to snap herself out of whatever lust-induced coma she was under. Seeing him half-naked was clearly affecting her state of mind. "I'll help you. I owe you that much, but just so were clear after we cast the spell, I'm done."

Holding his hand up in the sign of Scouts' honor, he proclaimed, "I'll keep my distance until you ask me to touch you."

"Then you'll be waiting forever," she said. The words were a big fat lie she was desperate to believe.

The mischievous glint in Lucifer's eye seemed to scream, good luck. "There's a reason why we can't cast it now. To complete the spell, I need to have your real body here with me."

The thought of actually being in Hell effectively freaked her the hell out. "I can try to teleport myself here, but you know my magic has a mind of its own right now. What happens if my real body ends up in the vile woods or somewhere worse?

"Our bond allows me to bring you to me anytime I want."

The idea that he held that much power over her was intimidating.

"But I won't violate your free will without permission."

She genuinely wanted to help him, but she had a 50/50 chance of surviving the upcoming confrontation with Farrow and The Void. "I might not survive long enough to help you."

Walking over to her, he backed her into the wall before caging her between his massive biceps. She hated to admit it, but she liked having his body this close to hers.

"If you can teach the novice witches to harness their powers in time, I have no doubt you will succeed. But to sweeten the deal, I'll offer you this, help me first, and I'll show you how to siphon my power through our bond. With the power of Hell backing you, you should have no problem stomping out that Earth elemental and whatever evil created it."

It was a shitty deal. "If you really care about me, then why aren't you offering your power for free?"

"Because everything has a cost, little witch, and this is yours!"

"Fine!" she called out as she tried to duck under one of his arms.

"Not so fast," he purred. "We have to seal the deal with a kiss."

Her soul was trying to pull her back to her body, but she fought against it. "Now you're just bullshitting..."

Before she could finish the sentence, he swooped in and claimed her lips with his own. Wanting to savor the taste of him forever, she willed her body to stay in the moment, but the kiss ended all too abruptly as her soul was whisked away. Sitting up in Faith's bed with a gasp, she touched her lips, which now felt cold and empty. Her emotions were all over the place, but as she sat there, with her heart racing, one thing became crystal clear. When this was all said and done, she wasn't so sure she wanted Lucifer to leave her

alone after all.

CHAPTER 23

Sarin kept her promise of persuading Faith and Phoebe to help her with research, while Haven sent her soul into the ether to talk to the mysterious L. In all fairness, the other girls hadn't put up a fight. Since they all wanted the same thing, everyone was more than eager to help.

They'd been at it for over an hour, and her eyes were heavy from scanning the monotonous text that read like stereo instructions. "Do you guys understand any of this gibberish or how it might help us?"

"It's pretty simple, Sarin," Phoebe commented from her cozy reading spot in the recliner. "I think you're overthinking it."

She'd been reading the same line over and over again, and it didn't make any sense. "Really? Then enlighten me. What am I missing?"

Phoebe looked bored as she tried to explain. "I don't know anything about the specific sigils you saw on that tree, but this book tracks with what my mom mentioned earlier. Haven's mom told Faith that deciphering the sigils was the key, and my mom said we could potentially contain The Void but not end it, right? Well, this book says we can do that by balancing the elements. As far as I can tell, we need a representation of each element to make it work."

She was still drawing a blank. "But what does that mean in a practical sense?"

Phoebe rolled her eyes in a very teenage way. "It's talking about powers. I'm an air element; you represent spirit, and Faith is fire."

"So, you think it's referring to our elemental magic and not actual elements?" Phoebe was onto something, and Sarin felt a tiny blip of hope bloom inside her chest.

"Since this book is all about sigils and magic, I don't think it's referencing a literal handful of dirt or an actual cup of water. The specific page I'm on says that when the four elements become one, all things are possible." Phoebe said as she held up the book in question.

"But I'm a spirit witch and don't represent any of the four elements." Haven sensed something more in her, but she didn't understand what that meant.

"Okay, so maybe not you specifically," Phoebe said in a dismissive tone. "But my mom represents water, and Farrow has power over the earth."

Sarin felt a surge of frustration. "I don't think Farrow is in a team-building kind of mood right now, especially since The Void is controlling her. So, let's say, for argument's sake, that we find another way to get all four elements together. Then what?"

"There are five elements," Faith announced, interrupting her. "The book I'm reading mentions the fifth one. I don't know how old these books are, but maybe the one Phoebe's reading predates this one. I know the spirit wasn't always considered an element, but if The Void is as powerful as we think it is, we should use all five."

Phoebe perked up, "I think Faith's right. But here's the tricky part. The most powerful sigils are made from blood, so if I'm reading this correctly, we would need to draw our elemental sigils around The Void in our blood and then cast some kind of spell to activate them. This book depicts what all the sigils look like, except for spirit, but it doesn't mention the spell we need or how to make it all work once the sigils have been drawn."

Phoebe's idea was a long shot, but it was a start. "Faith, what do you think?"

Faith closed the book she was reading with a defeated look. "This book has the symbol for spirit, but even if we find the right spell, we're still one element short of a full deck. Short of stealing my mother's blood or finding another earth witch, we're still shit out of luck."

Sarin didn't want to put Faith in another compromising situation, but if they needed the blood of five different elemental witches to stop The Void, then getting Farrow's was the only option. "Stealing the blood is a good idea. I just don't know how we can make it happen without one of us getting killed."

"I'll do it," Fallon called out as she strolled into the room. "When we go back to the clearing, I'll lure her out and get the blood we need."

"I'll help you," Faith declared with a look of determination that Sarin had never seen before.

Fallon gave Faith an assessing look before uttering, "I'm sorry, Faith, but you're not proficient enough with your magic to face her just yet."

"Then let's change that," Haven stated as she made her reappearance known. "We all need to train, and we need to do it soon. I feel like time is running out."

Sarin felt it, too. Something in the pit of her stomach told her if they didn't stop The Void soon, the consequences would be catastrophic.

Haven took control of the situation, and Sarin was grateful for her cousin's direction. "Everyone pack a bag. We can bunk at my cabin tonight. I want to be close to the clearing if we need to act quickly, and the wards I have in place should keep us safe, at least for one more night."

As the other girls scattered, she met Haven's worried gaze with one of her own. "Did you take care of everything you needed with L?"

"I did. Thank you for keeping it between us."

"How long were you lurking in the hallway for anyway?" Sarin asked, half joking.

"Long enough to hear Phoebe's plan, and for the record, it's a stupid one, but what other choice do we have?"

Sarin envied Haven's resolve and imagined them becoming close, you know, if they didn't die. "You owe me the truth?"

Haven sighed. "I do, and you'll get it soon."

She wasn't surprised by the brush-off. Haven wasn't going to divulge anything until she was good and ready. "Fine. But for now, answer me this. When we first met, you said you sensed I was more than a spirit witch. What did you mean?"

Haven rubbed the back of her neck. "I'm not sure yet. You're a conundrum, you know. Sometimes, you scream your thoughts at me, but for all that mind yelling, I still can't tell what's simmering deep inside you. There's more there, so much more, but I can't answer your question until you let me see it all."

"If I don't know what it is, how can I let you see it?" Sarin asked in a strained voice. Their situation seemed increasingly impossible.

"I know it feels frustrating, but you had a huge breakthrough the last time we trained, and when you killed the doppelgänger, it unlocked another piece of your magic. If we have to balance the elements, we have to learn how to control our elemental magic first. Faith has a good handle on hers, but Phoebe is a loose cannon."

Sarin's mind was reeling. "If we survive this, then what?"

She couldn't imagine strolling back into her old life like nothing had changed. Fallon had used a spell to hide her mother's death from the authorities, but Huntsville was a small town, and sooner or later, people were going to start asking questions. Disappearing felt like the right choice, but where would she go? She had some money saved, but it wasn't enough to start a new life on.

"I'm not going to lie to you. The odds of us making it out of this alive are slim. So, here's some advice a good friend once gave me. Don't think about steps two, three, or four. Think about step one, complete it, and then move on, okay? What's step one, Sarin?"

"Get to the cabin." It was such a simple concept, but her raging anxiety made it hard to accept.

"You got it. Do that, Sarin and the rest will come later."

The rest was a shitstorm of unknowns, but Haven was right. For today, all she had to do was get her ass packed and out the front door.

Being petite had its disadvantages, and Faith cursed her short stature as she found herself uncomfortably squished between Phoebe and Fallon in the back seat of Haven's car. Lucky for her, the weather was cold this time of year, and she wasn't sweating yet. Still, the choking threat of claustrophobia threatened to swallow her hole. Talking a few breaths in through her nose and out through her mouth, she rolled her shoulders back to prove to herself that she could still move. She was still mulling over all the information they'd found in the filigree-covered book Haven had taken from the library, and for some reason, her mind kept circling back to the description of The Hamadryades. Since her mother had been transformed into a Dryad by dark magic, it would stand to reason that she wasn't immortal, but the lore in the book also said Hamadryades were tied to the tree they resided in, and Farrow was running around wild and free. Maybe the lore was wrong, or maybe it was all connected, and she was just missing some integral piece of the puzzle. Getting her mother's blood was another dilemma. Even if they got close enough to try, Farrow's skin was more like bark now and not as easily pierced as flesh. Fallon had her athame, but Faith wasn't sure the knife would be enough.

The mood in the car was tense as Haven drove them out of Huntsville and onto the open highway. The city had ordered a temporary evacuation while they investigated the electrical mishaps going on around town, and traffic on the interstate was thick. Even Haven seemed extra jittery as she inched the car through the bumper-to-bumper traffic. Phoebe's incessant TikTok scrolling wasn't helping, and Sarin looked like she hadn't slept for a week. Everyone was on edge. As they drove toward the cabin, one thing was becoming increasingly clear. If they couldn't turn her mother back into the raging psycho she'd been before becoming a Dryad, then they'd be forced to kill her. It was a lose-lose, and Faith knew no matter the outcome, her mother was already lost to her. The ache in her heart had her reaching over the front seat to grab her best friend by the shoulder. Sarin gripped her hand back, and in that moment, she felt grateful to have these four strong women by her side during this impossible time. The drive back to the cabin took an extra hour with all the traffic, and when they finally arrived, she practically crawled over Phoebe's lap in a mad dash to escape the confines of the car. She never thought she'd be happy to see the cabin again, not after her mother had attacked her out on the lawn, but her bladder screamed for release, and her limbs were stiff from being sandwiched in the middle seat.

The attack came out of nowhere. One minute, she was standing by the side of the car stretching, and the next, her body was being catapulted backward by an unseen force. Slamming into a nearby tree, Faith thrashed against her unknown attacker as vines shot up from the ground, winding themselves around her arms and legs. Phoebe was writhing under her own set of plantlike bonds a few trees over, and when she heard Haven scream, her blood ran cold. Turning toward her voice, she watched her cousin kick and scream as a giant grey wolf dragged her out of the driver's side seat. Pinning her down on the gravel driveway, it let out a menacing growl as it opened its massive jaws over her throat. Sarin and Fallon were the only two not being restrained, and when Farrow stepped free of the forest in her full Dryad glory, she heard Fallon gasp in shock.

"Sister?" Fallon asked on a shaky breath. "What did you do to yourself?"

Farrow did a little twirl to show off her new body. "You don't like it?"

Her mother's voice was so different now; it was deep and grave.

Sarin took a step toward Haven, and the wolf let out a guttural snarl in warning.

Faith strained under the grip of the vines, and they tightened in response to her movements. "You can fight this, Mom. Don't let The Void take you away from me!"

Her mother turned her animalistic gaze toward her, and when their eyes met, Faith realized there was nothing human left inside the vessel The Void had created.

Ignoring her plea, Farrow turned her sights on Fallon and Sarin. "Thank you for bringing her to me, sister. I might let you live now."

She heard Fallon order Sarin to run as she stepped in front of her, but Sarin didn't listen.

Clapping her clawed fingers together, she offered Fallon a compromise." Give her to me, sister, and we can be together again."

"Not going to happen!" Fallon declared as she stood her ground.

"Fine!" Farrow huffed, "Then I guess I'll be getting a two-for-one."

Farrow darted past Fallon in a blur of motion. Swiping out her clawed hand with lightning speed, she backhanded Sarin so hard it sent the girl flying across the lawn. Landing in an awkward heap several feet away, her cousin remained motionless. With Sarin out of the way, Farrow began to circle her twin with an evil glint in her eyes.

"Fight it, Farrow! Then we can all get what we want," Fallon pleaded.

Farrow laughed, and the sound was filled with malice. "We don't want the same thing, sister. We never did. That's why I kept the truth from you.

You're the weak link with all your morals and feelings. Those petty things only blind you to our birthright. Our mother tried to harness the power of The Void for herself, and she would have succeeded had it not been for our bitch of a sister. Now, The Void has chosen me, and it won't let me go. Not until I end the ones who want to stop it."

At the mention of Haven's mother, Faith braved another glance in her cousin's direction. The wolf still had her pinned in place, but it hadn't made any moves to harm her.

"Then I guess there's nothing left to say," Fallon proclaimed as a ball of water materialized in her right hand.

"You think your little water magic is enough to stop me? Look at what I've become," Farrow mocked as she stretched out in her full Dryad form.

"All I see is a monster. Anything that was left of my sister died the moment you accepted The Void."

"I can kill them now, you know?" Farrow taunted. "Let me take Sarin, and the rest of you can live."

The move was well-played and made Fallon pause. "I thought The Void wanted you to stop all of us. Why bargain with me at all?"

The question was a stall tactic. Deep down, Faith knew her aunt was holding on to the hope that some small part of her sister remained inside that horrific animal-like shell. She knew it because she was desperate to believe it, too.

Anger colored Farrow's features as she stomped her goat-like hooves in indignation, "Because I didn't agree to be under its control! If I kill Sarin, the rest of you will be too distraught to keep fighting, and I can go free. This is your last chance, sister. Give me the girl or die!"

A subtle movement on the lawn caught her eye, and a sense of relief washed over her when she saw Sarin's body begin to stir. Reaching into herself, she summoned her fire magic. If she set the vines on fire, maybe she could break free. Her left hand ignited, but when the vine holding it burned away, two more spouted up from the ground to take its place. Fallon's ball of water gained in size as Farrow circled her, but her aunt's hesitancy cost her. Farrow shot a dozen dark green vines from her palms that wrapped themselves around Fallon's midsection. The vines retracted back to Farrow, pulling her aunt across the lawn until the sisters stood nose-to-nose. Fallon gripped Farrow by her forearm, letting her ball of water spread out over the thick vines that made up Farrow's arms. The liquid lubricated the plant-like appendages until Fallon was able to slip free of Farrow's grasp. Then, to Faith's shock, Fallon punched her twin dead in the face.

Farrow's head whipped to the side as blood dripped from the fresh split in her upper lip. "I hope you enjoyed that."

Grabbing Fallon by the arm, Farrow twisted it at an awkward angle. The loud crack of bone was audible as Fallon fell to her knees, screaming in pain.

Faith felt the world fall away as her mother bent down and gripped Fallon by her neck.

"No!" she cried. "Don't hurt her!"

"It's too late for that!" Farrow crooned as she stared at her twin with contempt.

Fallon's lips took on a blue tint as her oxygen supply was cut off.

Phoebe struggled against the vines holding her. "Mom, you have to fight her! Don't you fucking give up! I need you!"

Phoebe's frantic words must have hit a nerve because, somehow, Fallon found the strength to lift her uninjured arm and grab Farrow by the wrist. A look of shock passed over Farrow's face as a gush of blood bubbled out of her mouth. It continued to stream from her eyes and nose as Fallon held on tight. It took Faith a second to realize exactly what was happening. Fallon was using her magic to control the blood inside Farrow's body. The show of power was impressive and frightening. Faith had no idea her aunt was capable of something like that, and from the look on Fallon's face, neither had she.

Sarin had made her way to a sitting position, and when their eyes met, Faith watched her best friend slam her hands into the ground. The shock wave Sarin set free blasted its way through the earth until it erupted over Haven's body in an explosion of dirt, knocking the wolf off of her. The second Haven was free, she let loose a stream of fire that set the wolf's fur ablaze. The beast's glowing red eyes promised revenge as it yelped and ran for the cover of the woods. As Fallon continued to siphon the blood out of Farrow's body, the vines holding Faith loosened. Phoebe's squirming indicated the same was true for her.

"This isn't over!" Farrow snarled before disappearing into thin air.

Once Farrow was gone, the vines encircling Faith vanished. Following behind Phoebe, they made a dash toward Fallon. Phoebe got there first, and Faith's eyes misted over as she watched them embrace. Thinking on the fly, she picked up a small potted plant from the front porch stoop and dumped it out on the ground. Using the pot to her advantage, she scraped it across the blood-stained grass to scoop up as much of Farrow's blood as she could.

"Good thinking," Fallon praised with a pained grunt.

"I didn't know she could teleport," Faith admitted in a rush of words. She was riding high on adrenaline.

"I saw her do it the night I followed her into the woods behind your house," Fallon admitted as she cradled her injured arm.

Phoebe was visibly shaking as she tried to help her mother get up. "Let's get you inside. Can you walk?"

Shooing her daughter away with her good arm, Fallon stood without any assistance. "I'm not an invalid, Phoebe! It's just a broken arm!"

"You see where I get it from?" Phoebe commented sarcastically.

Sarin limped toward them, sporting a fresh black and blue bruise across her cheek, but the rest of her seemed no worse for wear.

Haven had her eyes glued to the tree line as she ushered Sarin over. "That could have been a hell of a lot worse! Once we get you two patched up, we need to get our shit together. I'm talking twenty-four-hour training and sleeping in shifts. That attack just proved how unprepared we are."

The ominous tone in Haven's voice terrified Faith. They weren't ready, and in order for her to get there, she had to let go of the hope that her mother was coming back to her. If today had taught her anything, it was that her mother and the monster were now one and the same.

CHAPTER 25

The mood was somber inside the crowded living room of Haven's rental cabin as they wallowed in defeat. A few days ago, Haven had been alone in these woods searching for her mother, and now, she had four new family members taking up residence in her private space. The irony that none of them were the person she'd come here to find wasn't lost on her. Sitting on the floor, she leaned her head against the soft cushion of the couch. She needed a minute to re-center herself after using a huge amount of her magic to heal Sarin's face and Fallon's broken arm. The girls had decided as a group, or newfound coven as Faith had deemed them, that the best plan of action was to scope out the clearing first and then return to the cabin to train. She disagreed. It was way too risky to put these untrained witches that close to The Void, especially after they'd just gotten their ass handed to them by Farrow. Fallon was being particularly stubborn on the issue and insisted on seeing the clearing for herself to better assess what they were dealing with. The others agreed, so Haven had officially been voted off Safety Island in a game of majority rules. It was one thing to help her cousins hone their powers, but now, she felt responsible for them. They were in a high-stakes game of life and death, and she knew going to the clearing was the wrong decision. The three girls in question were currently nose-deep in the books they'd taken from the library, searching for any clues that might help them figure out the correct spell to activate the sigils.

"Let's get this over with," Fallon exclaimed as she pulled her coat on over her newly healed arm.

Haven hated this reckless plan. It would be much safer for them to stay here and train until they were ready to place the sigils. "I still think the girls should stay behind."

"We've been over this," Fallon stated in a dismissive tone. "Staying together is the best option."

She didn't like being told what to do, especially by someone who was making rash decisions under extreme emotional duress. "You've been my aunt for a total of five minutes, so you don't have the right to tell me what to do. And if you care about the safety of those girls, then you should take my concerns seriously. You've already seen what your sister is capable of, but you haven't felt the power of The Void."

Staring over at Phoebe, Fallon shook her head in resignation. "You're right."

"What!" Phoebe huffed. "You're sidelining me again?"

"Is this what all teenagers are like?" she asked with a raised brow.

Sarin and Faith laughed at the comment, but Phoebe was less than amused. "You don't know me well enough to tease me yet, so shut it, Haven!"

She raised her hands in defeat. "I hear you, but no one is sidelining you. If we all die today, then what's the point of any of this? Aside from keeping you safe, I need some of you to stay behind to research. Think of it as a balance of resources."

Phoebe's brow furrowed as she looked between her mother and Haven, but when she finally spoke, her tone was softer. "I don't like all your wise old lady-speak, but I am awesome at research. And just so we're clear, I'm choosing to stay behind and not doing it because you told me to. You're welcome!"

The girl had some whit about her. If the teen managed to stay alive, Haven knew she'd become a formidable witch someday.

"I'll stay with her," Sarin offered. "I'm not ready for another encounter with Farrow. Not yet."

Faith walked over to the door and began lacing up her tennis shoes. "Well, I'm going, and no, I don't want to hear any pushback from any of you. If my mom tries to attack us again, I might be the only one who can reach her."

Haven doubted that especially since Faith had failed to do that very thing just hours earlier. Since there was no changing their minds, Haven begrudgingly followed her cousin and aunt out into the woods.

•••

Haven watched as Faith circled the tree that held the raised markings they now knew were sigils. Her cousin's eyes were full of wonder as she ran her hands up and down the trees rough bark. Leaving her to investigate, Haven motioned for Fallon to keep following her. The clearing was only a few feet away, and Faith was in earshot.

"It's just a big dirt hole," Fallon remarked as they approached the clearing—or The Void, as Fallon had coined it.

Haven had heard this all before, "You were expecting something else? Like a big gaping portal or a mystical, magical ball of light?

Fallon shrugged, "Well, yeah, kind of."

"You, of all people, know that magic can glamour itself. Maybe it's hiding what it really looks like. Easier to lure in your prey when your appearance is unassuming."

Shaking her head, Fallon paced back and forth. "I just can't believe Farrow found it after all this time. We've been searching for it for almost two years."

Haven meant to warn her aunt not to step over the line that separated the grass from the burnt circle of earth, but her words came too late. Fallon had barely placed a toe inside the clearing when Haven saw her body freeze in place. Reaching out, she tried to pull her aunt out of the circle, but when her hand connected with Fallon's body, the world around her faded into a wash of gray. The vibrant green of the forest bled into the desolate black landscape before expanding out and melding back together again. Haven's body was straddling the line of the two different worlds, and the feeling was disorienting. Scared of being taken over again, she pulled harder, and when Fallon finally broke free, her aunt fell to her knees outside the circle.

Trembling, Fallon mumbled, "What...what was that?"

Haven opened her mouth to try and explain, but Faith's panicked scream changed her focus. Running toward her cousin, she felt terrible for leaving Fallon alone to deal with the aftermath of the thrall of The Void, but her aunt was stronger than Faith, and she could hold her own if she had to. When she found Faith, the girl was staring over at the sigil-covered tree like she'd just seen a ghost.

Panting, Haven tried to catch her breath. "What happened?"

"It was right there!" Faith declared in a shaky voice. "I was trying to get a better look at that sigil near the top when an eye opened in the middle of the tree. It was right there, and it was staring at me. It's not there now, but I swear it was! Am I going insane?"

"You're not crazy, but I think this is our cue to get the hell out of here," Fallon announced as she limped over to them.

Fallon was still a little pale, and her hands were shaking.

"So, you believe me?" Faith asked as she slowly backed away from the tree.

"I do. I just got my own taste of what's lurking inside that clearing, and Haven's right. We're not ready. We should go back and regroup before we spend any more time here."

She let Faith lead the way back to the cabin so she could check in with Fallon. "Do you want to talk about what you saw?"

"Later!" Fallon replied in a hushed tone. "I don't want to freak Faith out any more than she already is."

Haven felt like laughing at the absurdity of that statement. "All things considered; I don't think that's possible."

Rubbing her hands over her arms, Fallon's expression turned soft. "I'm sorry about your mother, Haven. I wish I'd had the chance to meet her—and you—before all of this."

She wasn't sure what Fallon had seen inside the gray place, but she didn't need an apology from her. "I appreciate the sentiment, but your apology doesn't change anything. I know you didn't cause this, but you have the power to fix it by helping me train those girls. Can you do that, Fallon? Will you help me?"

Fallon nodded. "I should have listened to you in the first place."

The words were nice sentiment, but Haven didn't care about being right. All she cared about was keeping everyone alive.

CHAPTER 26

The sun hung low in the cloudy sky as the girls assembled outside the cabin, awaiting Haven's instructions. Being out in the open was dangerous, especially after the last two attacks, but they couldn't train indoors. Fallon had placed a few wards around the small side yard to try and protect them, but Haven wasn't convinced they would stop Farrow if she came for them again.

She had no idea where to begin, but since Phoebe was the most unskilled, she called her out first. "Have you been able to call your air element on purpose yet?"

Phoebe shook her head as she stepped forward to meet Haven in the middle of the semicircle the other girls had created. "No. It's still too new."

Haven understood that, and under normal circumstances, she'd tread lightly, but it was time for a crash course. "How did you feel the last time you wielded it?"

"Angry!" Phoebe blurted out without hesitation.

"And what makes you feel angry right now? I want you to visualize it and tell me what picture comes to mind."

As Phoebe closed her eyes, the wind rustled through the trees. "I see a picture of Selene's face, and I'm angry that I'll never get to see her again."

She knew this was going to be hard for Phoebe, but she needed to push her. "Now, picture the thing that took her away from you."

"What are you doing, Haven? "Fallon asked in an accusatory tone.

"Trying to teach her how to tap into her power as quickly as possible. We don't have time for hand-holding."

Phoebe's raven-colored hair danced around her face in thin wisps as the wind picked up.

"That's good, Phoebe, really good," Haven praised.

The next part was tricky. Phoebe needed to let her emotions guide her magic without allowing herself to get pulled under the onslaught of those same feelings.

"Imagine the doppelgänger is in front of you. What would you do?"

The leaves and foliage around Phoebe's feet lifted off the ground and began to circle her body in a chaotic air ballet.

"You guys might want to hold on to each other. I think it's about to get windy," Haven suggested to the other girls. All their gazes were locked on Phoebe.

Phoebe continued to twist and shape the air until a small funnel cloud appeared in the middle of the circle.

A sense of pride filled her heart as she watched the teen harness her magic. "Open your eyes, Phoebe."

Phoebe obeyed, and the gasp of wonderment she let out when she saw the small cyclone she'd created was a thing of beauty. To up the stakes, Haven tossed a ball of fire into the center of the tornado. The wind snubbed the flame out quickly, but the distraction cost Phoebe, and the funnel cloud spun out of control. Faith didn't have time to move out of the way before the windstorm plowed into her, knocking her on her ass.

"Ow! That hurt!" Faith yelled from the ground.

Haven managed to stifle her laugh, but Sarin couldn't control herself, and that earned her some serious side-eye from Faith.

Phoebe looked like she wanted to throw up. "Faith, I'm so sorry! Haven, why did you do that? I was doing so well."

"You have to be ready for anything, Phoebe. That monster won't give you a free pass next time."

She saw Faith cringe at her use of the word monster, but the sooner Faith got on board with what they were really dealing with, the better. "I'm sorry, Faith, but that thing isn't your mother anymore."

Faith dusted off her jeans before marching towards Haven with a pissed-off look on her face.

"You think I don't know that! My mother is my responsibility, and I won't let anyone else get hurt!"

Faith's hands filled with flames as she shouted. Apparently, Phoebe wasn't the only one who drew power from anger.

Haven took a few steps back. "Douse the flames, Faith! They're getting too big."

Faith hadn't noticed, but her flames had spread to her arms. Fallon used her magic to create a pocket of rain above Faith's head, and as the water poured down, her flames fizzled out.

"What the hell, auntie?" Faith was literally steaming as she turned her wrath on their aunt. Fallon didn't back down, and Haven was happy to let her deal with her niece's magical temper tantrum.

"Calm down, Faith! Your powers are reacting to your emotions. I know this is hard to accept, but I need you to be strong."

Faith's eyes misted as she crossed her arms over her chest. Haven didn't want to put a pause on training, but it was clear that Faith needed an emotional reset. She'd seen the surprise in her cousin's eyes when the flames had spread to her arms, and she wondered if the power boost was The Void's influence or a natural progression of the Faith's power.

"Faith, can you take Phoebe inside for a little bit? I think you both need a minute to calm down, and you could use a dry set of clothes."

"Fine," Faith conceded." I have to pee anyway."

Phoebe seemed too dazed to argue as Faith ushered her back to the cabin.

"Sarin, you're staying with me," Haven proclaimed.

After the other girls were out of earshot, she refocused on Sarin. "I saw what you did with the wolf. Can you do it again?"

The amount of power Sarin had pushed into the earth was impressive, but she needed to learn how to hone it.

"I'll just be over here," Fallon said as she sat on the front porch steps, presumably to watch the show.

Sarin shook out her hands. "Last time, I acted on pure instinct. I'm not sure I can re-create it now."

If Sarin needed motivation, she could work with that. Shooting a ball of fire at her leg, Sarin didn't react in time to avoid getting singed.

"What the actual Fuck, Haven?" Sarin yelled as she gaped at the fresh burn mark on her jeans.

"You needed incentive, so I just gave you some."

She heard Fallon snort from her spectator spot on the porch.

"If you think you can do better, feel free to jump in," Haven proposed. If her aunt didn't like her training tactics, she was welcome to take over.

To her surprise, Fallon got up and marched her ass on over. Haven knew Sarin had some unresolved issues with their aunt, and when she saw her cousin blanch, she wondered if this was a good idea.

"Are you okay with this, Sarin?"

Sarin's posture was tense, but she nodded in agreement. Tapping out, Haven left the circle to let Fallon take the lead. Her aunt didn't waste any time, and when Sarin's body clenched up like she was having a seizure, she knew Fallon was using the same magical method she'd used on Farrow.

"Stop!" Sarin cried. "It hurts!"

"Stop me yourself!" Fallon demanded.

She considered stepping in, but she hadn't shown Faith or Phoebe any mercy. Sarin needed the same push.

Still, she couldn't stand to see her cousin in pain. "If she doesn't fight back in the next thirty seconds, ease up Fallon."

Fallon kept it up as Sarin continued to struggle.

She knew her cousin had more in her. "Are you just going to stand there and let her hurt you? You deserve more than that after all you've been through. Fight her, Sarin!"

Sarin let out a strangled cry as a thin line of blood trickled from her nose. "Stop, please!"

Haven was about to tell Fallon to do just that when a massive shockwave blasted into both of them. The force of the blow was so strong it sent her flying across the lawn. Rolling onto her side, she had to shake her head a few times to stop the loud ringing in her ears. Fallon seemed equally dazed as she dusted herself off. Staring over at the livid look on Sarin's face, Haven couldn't help the smile that bloomed. Her cousin was turning out to be a formidable witch, and maybe, just maybe, they had a chance at surviving this after all.

CHAPTER 27

Dinner was three boxes of Kraft Mac and Cheese, and a handful of Ritz crackers Haven found in the pantry. During all the chaos, she hadn't thought of stopping supplies, and now most of the stores were closed due to the evacuation order. Faith said her house was stocked, so they could always drive over there to pick up provisions if push came to shove. After their intense training session, all the girls were giving her the cold shoulder. Their behavior was childish. In the grand scheme of keeping them alive, hurt feelings were inconsequential, but the shade still stung. Picking at her food, Haven tried and failed to act like the brush-off didn't bother her.

The cabin's tiny living room had been transformed into a dormitory, with blankets, pillows, and couch cushions strewn about to form a group of makeshift beds. She'd even offered up the empty side of her bed, but none of the girls had taken her up on it. It was their loss if they couldn't get over themselves enough to enjoy the comfort of a cozy bed over the hard floor. Dumping her paper plate into the garbage, she decided to turn it in for the night and let them stew in peace. Nothing she said or did right now was going to help. They'd either accept her training methods or suffer the grave consequences.

"I'm heading to bed. If you guys need anything, let me know."

"Night," Faith uttered under her breath.

The rest of the group ignored her. Shutting herself inside her bedroom, she felt more alone than she had in a very long time. Settling into bed, she was surprised at the soft knock on the door.

Maybe one of them had finally come to their senses. Pulling the warm fleece blanket over her legs, she said, "Come in."

She was surprised to see it was Fallon who came in and closed the door behind her.

"I hope you're a heavy sleeper because I snore."

"I'm not staying," Fallon declared as she leaned against the dresser. "Phoebe made a bed for me next to hers. I just wanted a few minutes alone with you to talk about what happened out there."

"Did The Void take you to that empty gray place?"

Fallon shivered at the mention of the alternate realm.

"It did," Fallon responded with a curt nod. "And I saw your mother. She came to me and told me what happened to her."

That little knowledge bomb got her blood pumping. "And?"

Fallon seemed uncomfortable as she shifted her weight from one leg to the other. "When your mother left you and your father all those years ago, she came back to this place to try and find some closure. Even though she killed your grandmother in self-defense, the guilt was still a heavy weight on her soul. She thought coming back here and facing her demons might help her move on, but when she arrived, the coven was long gone, and when she stepped inside the clearing, The Void sent her to that dark place. The Void wanted to use her, but when it realized she would never bend to its will, it decided to keep her trapped as punishment. That place is like a world between worlds, and your mother has been in a kind of stasis all this time. The Void hoped to sway her to its cause in time, but when Farrow came along, it jumped at the chance to manipulate another powerful witch from our lineage."

"She's alive? She's just been trapped in there this entire time?" Haven asked, feeling heartsick. "She never meant to leave us?"

"No, she didn't," Fallon said softly.

Fallon took a step toward her, but Haven shook her head. She didn't want to be touched right now, especially by someone who was basically a stranger. Fallon got the cue and backed off.

"Do you think we can get her back?" If The Void doesn't need her anymore, why won't it let her go?"

Fallon looked away. "I don't understand what The Void really is, or what its motives are. We know they're not altruistic, and the place it created is far beyond my understanding. I've never encountered magic powerful enough to create a pocket realm like that, if that's even what it is."

"That's not comforting," Haven remarked. She'd met a lot of powerful beings in her time, but aside from God, none of them held the power to create alternate realms.

"I know it's not what you wanted to hear, but I don't want to lie to you. That's not the best way to start a relationship, especially when ours already feels strained."

"You're right," Haven admitted. "I just wish I could catch a break. I'm sorry I haven't been more welcoming to you, but Sarin didn't have anything nice to say about you when we first met, and this new family dynamic is going to take some getting used to."

Fallon reached for the doorknob but paused. "It's strange for me, too, you know. My sister has guided me for most of my life, and I always believed in her. Realizing it was all a lie is a hard pill to swallow. Someday, I hope I can make it up to you girls, but you're right, it's going to take time. I'm a patient woman, Haven, so if we survive this, I believe we can move forward."

"I hope we can, too," she said, and meant it.

"Why don't you get some sleep, and maybe tomorrow we can start fresh?" Fallon offered as she left the room, leaving Haven alone with more questions than answers.

•••

After Fallon left, Haven fell into a deep sleep that took her back to the misty, empty, gray place where The Void had trapped her mother. Taking in the bleak surroundings, it was impossible to believe that her mother had been trapped in this land of nothing for over fifteen years, never aging, never changing.

"It hasn't been all bad," her mother's voice whispered from behind her.

As Haven turned, she took in the sight of her mother's beautiful face. It was a mirror of her own, and her heart ached for all the years they'd been denied. Sprinting into her mother's waiting arms, she held on for dear life. Their embrace was full of love, hope, and longing, and in that moment, Haven prayed her mother felt all of it. She wanted her to know how much she'd missed her presence in her life.

"How can you say that when you've been stuck here all this time?"

"You've been safe from The Void until now, and that's all that matters," her mother answered as she pulled back to stare at her.

They were the same height and build, and since her mother hadn't aged, they looked more like sisters than mother and daughter.

Haven was overjoyed at the reunion, but it felt too good to be true. "Is this real, or am I dreaming?"

"Does it matter?" her mother asked with a warm smile. "You're close, my love, so close to putting all the pieces together. I know the spell you need, but The Void will retaliate once I tell you. In this place, it knows all. Are you ready for what's to come?"

She was suddenly overcome with anxiety. Was she ready? Everything was happening so quickly, and right now all she wanted to do was slow down and embrace this moment with her mother. "I don't know. Maybe? What if I can't get the girls ready in time? What if we fail?"

"Take a deep breath, my love, and come closer."

As she leaned in, her mother whispered the words to the spell that could save them in her ear. The power behind them felt ancient and sacred. The ground rumbled under their feet. It was a manifestation of The Void's wrath.

"You have to go now, my love!"

Her mother stumbled away from her as the soil beneath their feet undulated in angry waves.

"I know you can stop the evil my mother set free so long ago. Believe in yourself, Haven! Believe in those girls!"

The wind howled as a deep chasm opened up in the earth between them. Fate was a cruel bitch to let her find her mother only to take her away again so soon.

"How do I get you out of here?" Haven yelled over the raging windstorm. "There has to be a way?"

Her mother blew her a kiss as her side of the chasm collapsed. "I love you, Haven. Tell your father I never meant to leave him behind."

"No!" Haven screamed as her mother fell into the gaping pit of black.

CHAPTER 28

Sarin was still upset with Haven for pulling that shit during training, but she'd be lying to herself if she said she wasn't impressed with what her cousin had coaxed out of her. Whether or not she could pull it off under an actual attack remained to be seen. Haven stumbled out of her room, looking like she hadn't slept in a week, and promptly shushed her on her way into the kitchen. Sarin hadn't known Haven for very long, but she'd already figured out her cousin wasn't much of a morning person. The last few days had been mentally and physically draining for all of them, but she knew the worst was still to come. They had Farrow's blood, so now, they needed to practice making their sigils. There was no telling what Farrow might do on the day they decided to take on The Void, so mastering them was essential. Practicing meant bloodletting, which Sarin wasn't looking forward to, but she didn't have a choice. To make things worse, they still hadn't found the correct spell to activate the sigils, which made all of this feel pointless. As the smell of fresh coffee filled her nose, an idea popped into her head. Walking into the kitchen, she dug around in the cabinets until she found a box of black garbage bags and some soup bowls.

"What is all that racket?" Faith grumbled from her makeshift bed on the couch. Her wavy blonde hair was a hot mess of frizz, and dark circles marred the pale skin under her eyes.

"I have a plan," Sarin replied as she carried the supplies into the living room.

"Unless you plan on being quiet, I don't want to hear about it," Faith proclaimed as she pulled the blanket over her head.

Ignoring her cousin's rude remark, she nicely asked Fallon and Phoebe to move out of her way. Her request was met with a lot of complaints from Phoebe, but a few minutes later, the living room was clear of all the bedding, and everyone was watching her with curiosity. Rolling the garbage bags across the floor, she grabbed both of the books depicting the sigils and asked Fallon to borrow her athame.

Sitting down on the flimsy piece of plastic, she motioned for the other girls to join her. "We need to practice drawing our sigils. We have to be able to re-create them on the fly, no matter what The Void throws at us."

"There isn't enough coffee in the world for this," Haven murmured from over in the kitchen.

"Haven, can you stand in for Farrow? Since this is just practice, I don't want to waste any of her blood."

Haven strolled into the living room with her steaming cup of coffee in hand. "Faith and I both represent Fire, but the magic in my blood will help boost the spell, so I plan to participate now and the day of."

Sarin was grateful for Haven's help, even though she was still mad at her. Finding the sigil that represented the symbol for spirit, she took a deep breath and cut her palm with the knife. "Shit, that stings!"

Holding her hand over one of the small bowls, she let her blood drip into the shallow dish until she collected enough of it to draw the symbol with.

"Here. Wrap your hand with this," Phoebe said as she offered her a pair of black leggings. "What? They're clean, and this is desperate times and all."

Sarin had her doubts about their cleanliness, and thankfully, Haven reached over and used her magic to heal the cut on her hand before she was forced to use the wad of fabric as a tourniquet. Dipping her index finger into the bowl, she carefully drew the symbol for spirit on the surface of the garbage bag before passing the knife and the remaining bowls to the other girls.

"I'm all about the magic but sharing that dirty-ass knife is just gross," Phoebe huffed as she wiped the blood-coated metal off on her jeans.

"Says the girl who handed me yesterday's pants to cover up an open wound."

"Whatever! If one of you gives me the herps, I swear I'll put a curse on you."

"You can't get herpes from blood, Phoebe. So just stop whining and do it already!" Faith spat. The girl was clearly not in the mood for any bullshit today.

Phoebe did as she was asked, but she bitched and moaned the entire time. The girl was an enigma. Haven was the last one up, and when she drew the sigil for Earth on top of the makeshift altar, all the other sigils lit up with an otherworldly glow. The sigils pulsed until the cabin exploded in a bright wash of light. Closing her eyes to avoid being blinded, Sarin's mind was overrun with images of Haven's life. The memories and secrets Haven had been hesitant to share were now on full display behind her closed lids.

She saw Haven and her friends save the world multiple times over. She witnessed the wins, and the faces of the people Haven had lost along the way. It was all there, laid out in scene after heart-wrenching scene. She saw monsters far more powerful than the doppelgänger or Farrow. And then she saw the blood. There was so much blood and loss that she felt like she might drown under the weight of it all. Then Lucifer's face came into view, and she finally understood who the mysterious L was. Haven had endured so much, come so far, only to have her life put on hold once again.

She could have walked away from Sarin the moment they'd met, but she hadn't. Instead, this strong woman had chosen to stay, chosen to walk hand in hand with them through another horrible storm. The mind meld faded as quickly as it had come on, and when she opened her eyes, she finally saw Haven for who she really was. Her cousin was a warrior and a powerful witch. A daughter who would stop at nothing to find her mother. She was a steadfast woman who would do anything for the ones she loved, and Sarin envied her. The room had fallen eerily silent, and as Sarin looked around at the faces of her family, she realized they'd all witnessed the same thing.

Haven was sweating as she stared down at the blood on her hand. "I, I don't know what..."

"It's okay!" Sarin cried out as she reached for her cousin. "It's okay. We're all here."

The other girls crowded around them as Haven broke down.

Stroking the hair away from Haven's face, she finally understood why her cousin had been hesitant to tell them the truth. "I get it now, Haven, and I'm in awe of your strength."

"Uh, guys, I appreciate the support, but you're kinda smothering me," Haven called out from inside the family cocoon. "Does this mean you forgive me for yesterday's training session?"

"I think it does," Sarin responded softly.

"That was a crazy ride! And I can't believe I'm saying this, but Lucifer's a total hottie! Like, when can I meet him?" Phoebe teased.

Leave it to the teenager to say some stupid ass shit in the middle of a heartfelt moment.

Leaning back against the couch, Haven took a deep breath. "I don't know what reaction I expected from all of you, but before I met Sarin, I never thought I'd be able to share my story with anyone. The people involved know, but who was I going to tell outside of them? I'm sure you have a million questions, but can we please put a pin in them until we've dealt with the crisis at hand?"

"So, Lucifer's the one who helped you find the book about Dyads?" Faith asked with a tinge of disdain in her voice.

"He's not what you think he is—at least not all of him," Haven shot back.

"Are you saying the King of Hell has a good side?" Faith questioned with a raised brow. "Why should we trust any information he helped us find?"

"You just saw everything, so you know why!" Haven snapped. "I know this is a sensitive subject because it involves your mother, but he's just trying to help."

The tension was rising, so Sarin cut in. "Let's not get off track. Haven, we saw what happened with your mother last night in your memories. Do you think the spell she gave you is real? Or was it just a dream?"

"Only one way to find out," Haven declared as she jumped up. "We should use a small amount of Farrow's blood and test it out."

"Test out what?" Fallon asked as she neatly folded the last of the blankets. "The spell is supposed to activate the sigils and contain The Void, so how do we recreate something like that?"

Haven paced around the small space. "We could let our powers get out of hand and then attempt to contain them using the spell and Farrow's blood."

Sarin watched Faith fiddle with the pendant on the end of her mother's necklace. "I'm all in for being prepared, but do you really think we should risk using any of Farrow's blood before we confront The Void? Can't we practice with Haven's again?"

Sarin was officially out of ideas.

"I don't know what just happened, but without the magic in Farrow's blood, we can't cast the balancing spell. Let's take the garbage bag outside since our sigils are already on it," Haven suggested.

"This idea feels like a long shot," Faith grumbled as she grabbed one end of the plastic sheet.

"Yup. This is totally dumb!" Phoebe added as she moved the bowls of blood out of the way.

"Stop complaining!" Fallon growled. "We're officially out of time, and we have to know if the spell is real before we go into that clearing again. If anyone has a better plan, speak up now."

When the room stayed silent, Haven motioned for Sarin to pick up the end of the bag closest to her, while Faith and Phoebe held the other end. Walking the bag outside, she was careful not to jostle the blood sigils that were still wet. After laying the bag down on the dirt, Faith pulled out the small potion bottle that held Farrow's blood. Faith had transferred it to the vial the night before.

"Are you sure about this?" Faith asked. "We don't have much of her blood to spare."

"We have to try!" Haven said in an encouraging tone.

Dipping her finger into the vial, Faith drew the sigil for Earth in her mother's blood. No light exploded this time, but the air around them seemed to tingle magic.

"What now?" Faith asked as she recapped the vial and handed it to Fallon.

Sarin was hoping for some direction from Haven, but the girl seemed lost in her thoughts.

"Haven?" Sarin pressed.

The question snapped her cousin back to the present. "Sorry. I'm just paranoid about being exposed out here. I don't think I'll ever be able to look at a wolf the same way ever again. Those mutated animals are just fucking creepy."

"Not as creepy as my mother turning into a Dryad!" Faith interjected.

Rolling her eyes, Sarin said, "This isn't a competition."

Haven's annoyance was noticeable, but to her credit, she didn't say anything else. "Faith, I need you and Phoebe to stand on opposite sides of the sheet, facing each other."

"You do know what you're doing, right," Sarin whispered to Haven under her breath.

Haven shot her with a fake-looking smile. "Not a clue but just go with it."

"Fallon, be prepared to douse Faith again if we need it, and Sarin, do you think you can deflect Phoebe's tornado with your shock wave if it gets out of hand?"

"I'll try, but why are you only using the two of them? Shouldn't we try something that involves all of our powers?" Sarin still wasn't convinced she could call her shock wave on command, and she felt like she needed to practice, too.

"Ideally, yes, but I need Fallon to monitor Faith in case something goes wrong, and I'm not sure your power will work with what I have planned."

Faith and Phoebe stepped into place, looking equally nervous.

"I want you both to pull out the same amount of power you did yesterday. Start small. Can you do that?" Haven asked as she motioned for the rest of them to take a step back.

A small flame erupted inside the palm of Faith's hand as a phantom wind blew through Phoebe's hair. They'd both been able to call on their elements without being goaded this time, and that was progress.

"See?" Haven teased. "My last lesson is paying off. Can you make them bigger?"

Faith raised her other hand, and when she did, her fireball doubled in size. It took Phoebe longer, but after a few minutes of intense concentration, the teen finally got the wind to rotate on a slow and steady spin.

"More!" Haven demanded. "Push harder!"

"I don't know if I can!" Phoebe cried.

"You can!" Haven urged. "Do it for Selene!"

Flames shot up Faith's arms the same time a fully formed tornado took shape in front of Phoebe.

The teen's eyes were wild as she stared at the huge cyclone. "Now what?"

Sarin saw the look of pride in Haven's bright green eyes as they watched the girls command their elements.

"Faith, I want you to toss a fireball into Phoebe's tornado. We need to merge the elements and throw them off balance before we try the spell."

The plan seemed dangerous, but Sarin trusted Haven.

"Are you sure?" Faith asked in a worried voice. The flames had spread past her elbows.

"Don't be afraid, Faith. Fallon's right here if we need to douse you again. Just let it all go!"

The flames receded down Faith's arms, flying straight into Phoebe's cyclone. On contact, the tornado erupted into a massive, twisting funnel of fire that teetered precariously between the two girls.

Grabbing Haven by the hand, Sarin motioned for the other girls to join them. Faith and Phoebe seemed happy to oblige as they sprinted away from the chaos they'd created.

"If you don't remember the words to the spell from our little mind walk, just repeat after me," Haven said as they joined hands.

Earth below and sky above,

Water flows, and fire is love,

Air that whispers, spirit bright,

Balance now, before our sight

As their words melded together in perfect harmony, Sarin watched the raging funnel of fire slowly shrink in size before fizzling out completely. Staring at the now empty space, she couldn't believe her eyes. The spell had been a success, which meant they still had a fighting chance against The Void. The win was short-lived. A loud buzzing sound rang out above them, and when Sarin looked toward the horizon, she saw a sight that scared the shit out of her. The bright afternoon sky turned a deep shade of midnight as a swarm of black insects headed straight for them.

"Get back to the cabin!" Haven yelled as she took Faith by the hand and ran.

Sarin didn't hesitate, and they'd barely made it back inside before the hailstorm of insects descended on the cabin. They covered all the windows and doors in a sea of spindly legs and wings.

"I dreamt about this," Haven admitted as she tried to catch her breath. "A horde of locusts came after me, but in the dream, they were inside the cabin."

"Locusts symbolize a spiritual awakening," Fallon revealed as she pulled Phoebe further away from the door. "Maybe the universe is trying to tell us something."

Just when Sarin thought one of the glass panels might explode under the weight of the writhing insects, the hissing and clicking noises stopped. "This feels like a bad omen."

Then, as if some unseen force had called them home, the locusts began to leave. They flew off the windows, one by one until tiny pinpricks of light returned to the cabin.

If Sarin knew one thing for sure, it was that Haven's ESP was always on point, even if the girl didn't recognize its meaning right away. "Haven, when did you have this dream?"

"After the first time I visited Lucifer," Haven admitted, looking a little shell-shocked.

"Do you think this has anything to do with him? Aren't locusts biblical in nature?" Sarin didn't know much about the Bible, but she vaguely remembered the Ten Plagues of Egypt having locusts.

"Maybe," Haven said absently. "I promised him I'd help him with the spell to find the Antichrist before we go to the clearing, so I think it's time I get that over with."

"Do you really think he'll give you the power boost he promised?" Sarin asked with a spark of hope. Surely, the power of Hell could do some real damage to The Void.

"I don't know, but if he does, maybe none of this other shit matters. Promise me you'll stay inside the cabin and try to get some rest until I get back?"

Sarin wasn't envious of what her cousin had to do, even if Lucifer was the epitome of eye candy. "We've got this, Haven."

"If something goes wrong down there and I don't make it back, I want you to know how much it means to me that I found you. All of you."

Sarin began to tear up at the threat of another goodbye. "I'm not ready to lose you just yet, so go, but make sure you come back so we can all die together fighting The Void, like one big fucked up happy family."

"Not funny!" Haven replied, lightly punching her on the arm.

Sarin knew it was a bad joke, but her cousin was about to venture into Hell to help Lucifer find the Antichrist, and she had no barometer for how to process that kind of information. All she could do was try to make light of the situation and pray that her cousin made it back safely. Because if she didn't, Sarin knew none of them were making it out of this alive.

CHAPTER 29

It felt wrong to leave the girls alone and vulnerable, but Haven reminded herself that a promise was a promise, and if she backed out of the deal with Lucifer, it might cost those innocent girls their lives. She was willing to pay the ultimate price to free her mother and stop The Void, but she couldn't speak for the rest of them. Sitting on her bed, she couldn't deny the twinge of excitement that flooded her at the thought of seeing Lucifer again. She'd tried to deny her true feelings for him, brushing them off as nothing more than a mix of adrenaline and stress. But now, with Adam out of the picture, she could easily tell the difference between her anxious feelings and the passion Lucifer brought out in her. He ignited something deep within her soul, something she couldn't explain, and those feelings terrified her more than Farrow or The Void. Closing her eyes, she sent her soul to the depths of Hell to find the one man that made her feel alive.

Throwing her essence into the ether, her feet touched down in the middle of a dark, cavernous space she hadn't been aiming for. Cursing her manic magic that had failed her once again, she tried to get her bearings in this unknown place. The massive underground structure was cave-like, with soaring ceilings covered in stalactites. The long, bony-shaped cylinders dripped onto the surface of a frozen stream, creating a crescendo of unnerving tap-tap sounds. She followed the petrified river through several bends until it came to an end at the mouth of an enormous frozen lake. Rising from the middle of the water sat a monstrosity of a chair that looked like it had been carved out from charred bone and obsidian. Lucifer's throne was a shimmering thing of nightmarish beauty.

"It's a bit ostentatious, don't you think?" Lucifer commented as he appeared beside her. Haven jumped at the sound of his voice.

He obviously enjoyed keeping her on her toes, but she didn't like being snuck up on, especially when she was in Hell. "Are you trying to give me a heart attack?

"If you died, I would be very, very unhappy," he replied in a sexy voice.

"Where are we?" she asked as a shiver ran over her skin—a shiver that had nothing to do with the temperature inside the cave and everything to do with the man standing next to her.

"We're in the ninth circle of Hell. This is the place where God banished me originally. But as you can tell from visiting my private chamber, I prefer a more comfortable setting for my day-to-day endeavors. However, this place holds the most power in all of Hell, so I wanted to bring you here to cast the spell."

He had a book tucked under his left arm, and she recoiled when she realized what it was. The Dark Book was the Bible's counterpart, and she knew from past experience just how dangerous it could be. The fact that he needed it for their spell made her wonder whether this was such a good idea after all.

"So, you're saying Dante's Inferno got most of it, right? That all the different rings of Hell really do exist?"

She felt like Alice trapped in a wildly fucked up version of Wonderland.

"In a sense, yes. Hell is made up of several realms, and this one is its black beating heart, where all the treacherous, most evil of souls are sent. The lake is called Cocytus, and watching over it has been the bane of my existence. The treacherous sons of bitches locked underneath the surface are quite resourceful, so a bit of warning, don't get too close to the water's edge. It might look frozen from this side, but things have been known to escape."

Haven cringed at the thought of what might be lurking underneath that glassy, unearthly surface. Turning away from the eerie lake, she followed Lucifer as he led her into another smaller cavern.

"I set up an area in here that I think will be more comfortable for our purposes."

Oversized black satin pillows were strewn about in the shape of a circle, and in the center, a blue-tinted flame danced on top of a pile of shiny black rocks. Despite their icy color, the strange flames warmed the small space. Lucifer walked to the corner of the room, where a large pentagram had been painted on the floor in thick white lines. After placing The Dark Book on top of the pedestal, he turned to face her. His eyes blazed a bright shade of red as they took her in, reminding her of the beast underneath the surface. He'd never hidden himself from her, and even though his real appearance unnerved her, she couldn't fault him for what God had turned him into.

"Come to me," he beckoned. "I need you to stand in the middle of the pentagram with me so I can bring your body here."

She swallowed down her fears as she stepped inside the circle to meet him.

"Ready?" he asked as he took her by the hand.

Pressing his palm against her branded one, he didn't wait for her answer. The searing heat that blasted into her body forced a scream from her lips, and then everything went to shit. Her awareness shifted back to the cabin, then to him, then back and forth, like a ping pong ball on speed. The erratic pulling sensation continued until she felt like she might split in two.

"Stop fighting me and let go!" he ordered.

She hadn't purposely been resisting him, but it made sense. Her subconscious mind knew Hell wasn't a safe space, and it was a lot easier to escape danger when all she had to do was blip her soul back to the safety of her body. Protecting her actual body from harm was an entirely different beast.

"That's it. It's almost over," Lucifer said softly as his warm breath fanned over her face.

The pressure around her body began to ease, and when she opened her eyes, Lucifer was staring down at her with a look of longing that she didn't quite understand. Their hands were still clasped, and his touch still felt electric, but now, the searing heat had nothing to do with pain. He lit up every part of her that she'd tried to deny until now, and with the threat of everything weighing down on her, she didn't want to fight the attraction anymore. Standing on her tiptoes, she wrapped her free hand around the back of his neck and pulled him down to meet her lips. The kiss was more sensual than anything she'd ever experienced before, and when he tried to pull away, she moaned in protest.

"If you keep kissing me like that, I won't be able to play nice."

"What if I don't want you to?" She couldn't believe the words that were coming out of her mouth, but if she was going to die soon, she wanted to have this experience with him.

He moved his hands down to grip her around the waist. "You need to be sure because once I touch you, I won't be able to stop. I've been waiting for you for far too long."

His sexy words solidified her choice. "I'm sure."

"Let me take you back to my private chamber, where it's more comfortable."

She thought back to the memory of him banging that other woman in his bed and shuddered. "No. I don't want to do this in a bed you've shared with anyone else."

"Fair enough," he said as he pulled his shirt over his head.

The sight of his chiseled chest had her heart racing. Threading his fingers through the back of her hair, he took her lips again. She needed more. She needed all of him. Placing her hands against his bare chest, she explored the curves of his body down to the waistline of his jeans. His skin was warm, and as she unbuttoned the top button of his pants, his breathy growl urged her on. Then, it was a whirlwind of hands, mouths, and discarded clothes before he laid her down on the pile of silky pillows. As he touched her, she forgot about the world above them. All that mattered was this moment and this beautiful man above her. Closing her eyes, she tried to savor it, but Lucifer gripped her chin and forced her to look at him. The act felt intimate, and she watched as a mix of conflicting emotions ran through his dark eyes as they took what they needed from each other. His body felt right inside of hers, and when she finally found her release, he was quick to follow. Lying beside him under the cave's grey-tinted ceiling, she wondered how she'd ever been afraid of him. Looking at him now, all she saw was a man, a very sexy man who was smiling at her like he'd just won the lottery. Staring into his dark, soulful eyes, she felt scared for a completely different reason. She was terrified of all the things he made her feel.

"What I would give to know what's going on inside that beautiful brain of yours, my little witch?"

Rolling onto her side, she faced him. "I'm thinking about how that ended way too quickly, and next time, I want to take my time with you."

"So, you're saying there's a next time?" he teased.

Smiling, she realized she really did want more time with him—more time like this when he was just a man, and she was just a woman—not a witch or fallen angel and all the responsibilities that came with those titles. "If I survive, we'll see."

His demeanor turned from playful to serious. "I'll do everything in my power to ensure that you do. If I could leave this place, I'd burn down the entire world to keep you safe!"

He'd done more than enough to earn her trust, and she believed him. Pulling her pants back on, she allowed herself to take one more look at his gloriously naked form, just in case this was the last time.

"Keep looking at me like that, and the spell will have to wait."

She wished she could hide here with him for a little while longer. "As much as I'd like that, I'm out of time, and the girls need me."

Lucifer reached for her. "What if I said I need you, too?"

She didn't know how to respond to that, especially when she had no choice but to leave him. Pulling on the rest of her clothes, she ignored his question and the strange sensation in her chest. "Do you know anything about locusts?"

The disappointment on Lucifer's face was palpable as he snapped his fingers and magically returned his clothes over his naked body.

Haven snorted. "If you could just do that, why all the clothes taking off?"

"Builds the anticipation. But to answer your question, I know that locusts are annoying little pests, but not much else."

"I had a dream about them after I visited you, and then a horde of them came after us at the cabin. Sarin mentioned their biblical reference, but with The Void in play, I don't know what to think."

"I'm familiar with the story about the Ten Plagues, and as much as God would love to take credit for them, it wasn't Him. They were nothing but a chain of strange and horrible natural phenomena."

Walking over to the altar he pulled out a small scrying mirror, a set of white and black candles, and what looked to be a star chart.

"In order to cast the spell, I need you to stand in the center of the pentagram and act as a conduit. I have access to celestial magic, but you have access to Earth magic. I need to channel both to find the location of the Antichrist."

He placed the white candle at the top of the pentagram and the black one at the bottom. "To represent light and dark. Whichever the Antichrist might become."

If this worked, they would know where and when the Antichrist would rise, and the idea of it coming to pass during her lifetime was terrifying.

"If the Antichrist is on Earth, the scrying mirror will reveal its location to us. If it's somewhere else in time or space, it will show up on my celestial map."

Lucifer took The Dark Book from the altar, before placing the mirror and the map on opposite sides of her feet. Stepping into the pentagram, he met her in the center, and she recoiled as the book's evil stain washed over her.

"I know you're immune to that thing, but it's making my skill crawl."

Placing a tender kiss on her forehead, he apologized. "I'm sorry. I have to read the spell from inside the pentagram, but I'll try to finish quickly. Give me your branded hand."

She held up her palm, and when their hands met, that same searing heat as before blasted up her arm. She wanted to pull back, but Lucifer intertwined his fingers with hers and held on tightly as he read the words to the spell out loud.

Stars above, so ancient and wise

Reveal to me the hidden lies

Through celestial light, the truth be shown

Reveal the one of shadow and bone

Show the visage cloaked in night

Unveil the source of endless blight

As he chanted, Haven's body broke out in a cold sheen of sweat. She didn't know if it had to do with the proximity to the book or the spell itself. A nauseous feeling churned inside her stomach until she couldn't hold it down any longer. Lurching to the side, she tried to avoid the mirror as she vomited repeatedly. Whatever evil Lucifer was channeling was making her physically ill. Wiping her mouth with the back of her hand, she felt disgusted with herself.

"Hold on! I'm almost done," he promised.

"Trying my best over here," her voice sounded raw, thanks to all the stomach acid coating her throat.

As Lucifer's words trailed off, the uneasiness inside her finally began to ebb. Panting, she was glad it was over. She needed to get back to the girls and take a scolding hot shower to scrub off the vile feeling of evil that coated her skin.

Lucifer pushed the sweat-slicked hair out of her face, and the kindness in his gaze threatened to melt her heart. "Thank you!"

"Sorry about the mess," she said sheepishly, referring to her not so small pool of vomit.

With a wave of his hand, it disappeared, along with the disgusting taste in her mouth.

The hair on her arms stood on end as another wave of evil skirted across her skin. "Now that it's over, do you mind getting that book away from me?"

After placing the godforsaken book back on its altar, Lucifer picked up the scrying mirror and gazed into its glossy surface. He turned the mirror right to left before placing it back on the ground. Then, he repeated the same action with the map.

"That's strange," he commented as he scrutinized the map with a confused look." We did everything correctly."

She had a bad feeling about this. "What's wrong? Can't you see where the Antichrist is?"

"That's just it," he said, turning the map toward her. "The Antichrist is nowhere and everywhere."

She felt dumbfounded as she stared at the very normal-looking map in his hand. "What am I looking at, exactly?"

"This map shows the construct of the cosmos outside of the Earth, and there's nothing on it, but when I look into the mirror, everything is illuminated."

"Is that good news or bad news? Maybe it means the Antichrist will never come to be?"

His shoulders slumped in defeat. "Then I'll never leave this place."

And they'd never get the chance to be together.

"Putting my personal feelings aside, I don't think that's what this means," he said as he tossed the map to the ground. "Since the mirror is showing a massive source of light, I think the Antichrist may be on Earth, but I don't understand why it can't pinpoint its location."

The piercing sound of breaking glass reverberated through the cave as the ground beneath her feet shook. Lucifer reached out to steady her as the tremors continued.

"Time for you to go! Give me your hand so I can keep my end of our agreement."

"What was that?" she asked in a shaky voice. The shifting movement of the ground threatened to resuscitate her nausea.

"Something broke free from the ice, and I need to send you back before it smells you."

He was the King of Hell, so why did he seem so panicked? "Isn't this your realm? Can't you just send whatever that is right back in?"

"Yes, but not without a fight. The souls in this realm are the strongest in all of Hell, and there's a good chance that whatever broke free is capable of subduing me for a short time. I'll recover, but you won't."

Wet shuffling noises echoed through the chamber as something large made its way down the passageway they'd come through.

"Hand, now!" he demanded, his voice sharp and insistent.

Raising her palm to meet his, she saw real fear in his eyes. "This is going to hurt. I'm sorry."

As he transferred some of his power to her, the brand on her palm burned like never before. Then, her entire body erupted with pain and light as his angelic essence was forcibly shoved into her. It was fire, burning and hot. It was vengeance for all that had been done to him. It was life, power, and the fuel she needed to save her family.

The pain receded, but he didn't let go of her hand. "Don't die, my little witch. I still have big plans for us!"

She knew it was time to go, but considering this might be the last time she ever saw him, she needed to tell him how she felt. "I want you to know that I see you now, not just the beast. I see the man you want to be, and I'll always be grateful for your help."

"That sounds like a goodbye, and I'm not ready for one," he said as he pulled her in for a scorching kiss that stole her breath.

"What did the story about Daphne mean in your letter? And the part about the tree and its roots?"

The monster let out a guttural roar that was too close for comfort.

"You'll know when it's time."

"Seriously, this again? Why do you always have to be so cryptic?"

His face lit up with a sexy smile. "It's a character flaw, what can I say?"

The beast finally made its way into the cave, and she blanched at the sight of it. It was humanoid in appearance, with black beady-shaped eyes and milky white skin that was covered in a slick sheen of ice. The thing had an oozing black scar that crisscrossed across its midsection, where it looked like it had been torn in half and then haphazardly sewn back together.

Facing Lucifer, Haven needed to get one last look at his handsome face. "I'll try not to die if you promise to kill that thing."

"Agreed," Lucifer said as the monster leaped for them.

CHAPTER 30

Faith woke to the sound of a loud thump. Haven had been gone all night, and while the other girls managed to get some restful sleep, hers had been fitful at best. Her dreams had been plagued with images of her mother's face morphing between her Dryad and human appearances, and it was unsettling, to say the least. Haven came barreling out of her bedroom, looking like she'd just gone to war. Her long red hair hung in tangled waves, and her clothes were a disheveled mess of wrinkles.

"Is everyone okay?" Haven asked in a rushed string of words

"I think the better question is, are you okay? No offense, but you look like shit."

Haven's eyes were wild as she smoothed a hand through her crazy hair, "Yeah, well, a trip to Hell will do that to a person."

There was a different kind of power wafting from her now. "Did he do it then?"

"Do what?" Haven asked as she turned on the coffee pot.

Faith wasn't sure if Haven was playing dumb or if her cousin was just completely out of it from her little road trip to Hell. "There's a new hum of magic surrounding you that wasn't there before."

Haven took a whiff of her T-shirt, and she couldn't stifle the laugh that escaped her lips. Her cousin was looking and acting like a total hot mess this morning. "You can't sense it?"

"No. I feel exactly the same. Let's just hope whatever he juiced me up with works because I have a feeling we're going to need all the help we can get."

The thought of facing off against her mother scared the shit out of Faith. Had The Void really corrupted the last tiny morsel of her human soul? Or was there still something left to redeem? Faith had a bad feeling she wasn't going to get an answer before she was forced to act. The other girls were quiet as they milled about the cabin, getting dressed and brushing their teeth as if this was just another typical day. That old saying about the calm before the storm was really hitting hard right now. Looking around at the faces of her family, Faith tried to focus on all the good things that had come along in her life. It was strange how the gravity of one bad situation had the power to erase years' worth of good memories. The line between the person she'd been and the person she was becoming had been drawn in blood, and she felt like she could what if herself forever. What if she'd never cast that spell with Sarin? What if her mother had never been turned into a Dryad? Questions like these would plague her for the rest of her life if she survived today. Sarin handed her a cup of coffee, and she sipped it in silence. It tasted bitter and stale—a perfect flavor match for her tortured soul.

"What's going on in that little blonde head of yours?" Sarin asked with a raised brow.

Faith knew what was coming next, and she didn't want or need the pep talk Sarin was attempting to give her. "You really don't want to know."

It wasn't that she didn't appreciate Sarin's concern. She did, but if she started talking about her feelings, she was going to shut down completely. Luckily, Haven broke the tension by announcing it was time to leave. Stuffing a duffle bag with supplies, Faith watched as Fallon tied the vial of Farrow's blood to a string around her neck.

Her aunt must have felt her gaze because she acknowledged her without looking in her direction. "I want to keep it close. Just in case."

Nodding, she followed Haven and Sarin out of the cabin. Fallon and Phoebe were close behind, and as they made their way into the thick woods, she took note of the ominous storm clouds brewing overhead. The dark grey skies set the appropriate mood for what they were walking into.

Every hint of shadow and every crunch of a twig had her jumping as they trekked through the dense forest to confront The Void and her mother. The morning dew was still fresh on the leaves as they walked in a tight formation, one behind the other. It was eerily quiet, like the woods knew what they were here to do and was offering one last moment of calm before the proverbial storm. As Faith passed the strange tree covered in sigils, she cringed at the memory of the frightening eye that had blinked at her.

"We're almost there," Haven called out from the front of the line. The girl was a natural-born leader. "Stay alert!"

As the woods opened to the clearing, Faith skirted around the burnt area that housed The Void. Things seemed calm, but she knew The Void had every intention of stopping them, it was only a matter of when. The girls took up their positions around the clearing and were setting up to draw their respective sigils when the earth inside the center of the clearing exploded in a blast of dirt and rock. Flailing, Faith tried to find her footing as gravel and earth rained down on them. The eruption was a warning bell that signaled the beginning of the end, and she felt her stomach drop as a group of mutated animals emerged from the woods behind the clearing. Closing in on them, their collective growls culminated in a haunting melody that made her skin crawl.

"Get away from the clearing!" Fallon called out as she backed up.

A giant white wolf led the charge, and it had its predatory gaze set on Sarin. Two other wolves flanked it; one with grey matted fur that sported a nasty red burn mark down its back and another smaller brown wolf that was foaming at the mouth. They were twice the size of normal wolves, with bright yellow eyes that glowed with malice. A huge black bear led up the rear, and it was the most horrific sight of them all. The skin around its mouth had been peeled away to reveal its teeth all the way back to its jawbone, and its body was covered in shiny red and black vines that resembled twisted muscle and tendon. As Faith took in their grisly, mutated appearances, she felt sorry for them. The Void had done this to them against their will.

"Stand together, as close as you can!" Fallon yelled as the white wolf leaped for Sarin.

Raising her hands, Fallon used her magic to create a protective wall of ice that rose up around them. The white wolf was quick and managed to jump over the top of the wall before it reached its maximum height. Faith was thankful for her aunt's quick thinking, but now, they were trapped inside an ice pit with a vicious. The white wolf paced in front of Sarin, snarling and snapping its massive canines in her direction.

I should have killed you the first day we met.

The warped and distorted human-sounding voice that came out of the wolf was a thing of nightmares, and Faith knew it belonged to her mother.

Farrow was nowhere to be seen, but she was using the wolf to do her bidding. The wolf reared back on its hind legs, but Phoebe called in her wind and blasted it into the side of the ice wall before it leaped. Shaking its massive head, it recovered quickly before making another play for Sarin. Blasting it with a ball of her fire, Faith stopped the wolf before it could reach her cousin. Yelping, it retreated to rub its signed fur against the cold wall of ice. The bear let out a terrifying roar of protest as it banged its massive paws against the outside of the barrier, and the ice rattled under its wrath.

"If it breaks through, I'll handle it," Haven called out as her hands filled with flames.

Fallon's piercing scream pulled her attention away from the injured wolf, and she blanched when she saw that her aunt was covered in a thick mass of vines. Farrow had used them to break through the ice and capture her sister, and as the vines retreated back to their owner, Fallon's body slammed into the ice wall, creating a human-sized hole. The impact was so hard it had Fallon spitting up blood as Farrow pulled her across the grass. The hole her aunt's body left in the ice made them vulnerable to the predators beyond, and the brown wolf didn't waste any time before attempting to dart inside. A massive blast of fire flashed in front of Faith's ace as Haven set the wolf on fire. It howled and pawed at its face before falling over into the grass, where it stayed.

Farrow had an evil gleam on her animalistic face as she pulled out a knife made of vines and stabbed it deep into Fallon's side. Staring through the hole in the ice, Faith felt frozen as she watched a river of blood gush down her aunt's side. Phoebe screamed in protest, but Haven held her back.

"Go to her. We've got this!" Sarin yelled as she let out a massive shock wave that slammed the white wolf into the ice wall. The impact was so hard it cracked the ice in half, and the wolf landed on the ground in nothing but a pile of fur and broken bones.

Fallon lifted her bloodstained arm, and the hole in the ice began to reseal itself. Running, Faith jumped through the opening before her aunt could close it completely.

"Go back!" her aunt screamed in a panicked-filled voice. "Go back, now!"

The bear and last remaining wolf ignored Faith as she ran toward her mother.

Farrow seemed pleased by her choice, as evidenced by the welcoming look on her face. "Come to me, daughter. Stand with me."

Her mother had changed even more since the last time she'd seen her, and the familiar shape of her face was now completely gone. "Let her go, Mother! She's your sister!"

Farrow ripped the vial of blood from Fallon's neck and stared at it with disdain. "Is this what a sister does? Steals my blood to try and stop the very thing I've waited my entire life for."

Throwing the vial to the ground, Farrow stomped on it with her cloven hoof, effectively shredding any last hope they had at defeating The Void.

"No!' Faith screamed as the weight of the moment crashed over her in a fresh wave of despair.

Farrow pulled the knife from Fallon's side and used it to stab her again. This time, in the shoulder.

"Run, Faith!" her aunt pleaded as her complexion turned pale. It's too late for me."

"Listen to her daughter. Join me."

Faith was so focused on her mother and Fallon that she didn't notice Haven's approach until the girl was standing right in front of her. Turning, she saw that Phoebe and Sarin had left the protection of the ice wall and were using their powers to keep the remaining animals away from them.

"Get out of my way, Haven! This isn't your fight." She was done letting other people fight for her.

Haven grabbed her by the arm. "He told me I would know when it was time."

Struggling against her hold, Faith didn't understand. "What are you talking about? Just get out of my way! Can't you see she's killing her?"

Farrow shot a vine at Haven, but her cousin deflected it with a ball of fire.

"Faith, look at me," Haven demanded. "Look at me now!"

Faith let her anger take control, and when her flames exploded from her hands and spread up her arms, Haven had no choice but to let go. Farrow used the distraction to her advantage and struck Haven with another set of vines. The insidious appendages wrapped themselves around Haven's neck, yanking her to the ground. Faith was about to step in when something strange happened. Haven's bright green eyes turned a burning shade of red, and her entire body erupted in wild blue flames. The flames quickly burned away Farrow's vines, and her mother hissed as they disintegrated into ash. Rising, Haven rolled her shoulders as the power Lucifer had given her manifested itself.

As Haven faced off against Farrow, she yelled back, "The tree, Faith. You have to destroy the tree with the sigils. That's what Lucifer's note meant. Farrow and the tree are connected, and a tree can't survive without its roots."

The blue flames surrounding Haven's body converged into a single ball of flame that she held in her hand, and when she tossed it at Farrow, it knocked her a few feet away from Fallon. The tree in question stood only a few feet behind her mother. It had fascinated Faith since the first time she'd come into these woods, and if Haven's theory was correct, maybe she really had seen an eye in its trunk—her mother's eye. There was no time to ponder it or question why The Void would bother to bind her mother to the tree. Right now, all she wanted to do was save her aunt's life.

Farrow regained her composure quickly, and when she clapped her clawed hands together, a murder of mutated crows came barreling out of the forest. They descended on Haven, attacking with a fever her cousin couldn't keep up with. Haven ignited in those strange blue flames again, and her fire disintegrated any of the birds that dared to touch her. With Haven occupied, her mother closed in on Fallon. Grabbing her sister by the back of her hair, Farrow sliced her claws across her sister's cheek. Rage burned inside Faith as she flung a fireball at her mother in a desperate attempt to get her away from Fallon. She wasn't sure if her aunt could survive the wounds she'd already sustained, but she knew if Farrow stabbed her one more time, it was game over.

"No, Phoebe, stop!" Sarin yelled.

Turning, Faith saw Phoebe running toward them with a look of desperation in her eyes. The gray wolf was nowhere to be seen, but Sarin continued to blast the bear with her shock waves. If Phoebe got too close, Faith knew Farrow would hurt her, too. Staring between the monster that had once been her mother and her aunt, who was bleeding out on the ground, the choice was made simple.

"Join me, daughter, and The Void will give you all you've ever dreamed of."

The tears she'd been holding finally spilled over. "I just want my mom back. Can it give me that?"

Her mother laughed at her. "You give me tears? You've always been weak. I'm offering you unlimited power, and you give me this. You're pathetic."

"I'm stronger than you think," Faith countered as she blasted a fireball past her mother right into the sigil-covered tree.

The effect was immediate, and as the tree went up in flames, Farrow screamed in agony. Grabbing her aunt, Faith gently pulled her out of the way as Farrow fell to the ground. Her mother rolled and hissed as she tried to extinguish the non-existent flames on her body. As Farrow writhed in pain, the green and brown vines that were now her skin withered as the tree behind her burned with a fiery vengeance. Embers and ash rose all around Farrow's body as the life The Void had bound to the tree was extinguished. Holding on to her aunt, Faith sobbed as the charred remains of her mother stopped moving. Farrow was dead. The mythical beast The Void had turned her mother into was gone, and all that remained inside of her was a tsunami of grief that threatened to drown her.

CHAPTER 31

Haven's body vibrated with the force of Lucifer's power. Staring down at the strange blue flames that coated her skin, she watched in awe as the cuts and scratches left over from the crows healed before her very eyes. The power was new to her, but when she willed the flames to go away, they obeyed. Taking stock of the situation, she saw Sarin running towards them as the bear limped back to the forest. The moment Farrow's body stopped moving, the connection to the monstrous creatures had been lost. Farrow was dead, and Faith was sitting on the ground, rocking herself back and forth as she stared over at her mother's charred remains.

"Do something! Help her!" Phoebe cried as she knelt beside her mother.

Fallon was in bad shape. Pressing her hand against her aunt's chest, she chanted the words to the familiar healing spell three times, but nothing happened. Staring down at her hands in confusion, she wondered if this was The Void's doing or if using Lucifer's power had tapped her out completely.

"What's wrong, Haven? Keep going!" Phoebe begged between sobs.

Frantic to try and save the aunt she'd just met, Haven tried again and again. "It's not working."

The sky began to darken, and the wind howled in response to Phoebe's pain.

"We have to finish what we started. It's the only chance we have at saving her."

If The Void was responsible for her unpredictable powers, then closing it was the key to getting her healing magic back.

"Farrow's dead, and the vial of her blood is gone, so screw The Void. We need to get my mom to a hospital now!" Phoebe screamed.

The ground shook as a kaleidoscope of light erupted from inside the clearing.

"I don't think The Void is going to let us leave," Sarin stated with a wild look in her eyes.

"How do we close it without her blood?" Phoebe asked as she held onto her mother, who was turning paler by the second.

Staring into the faces of her cousins, she knew they were all counting on her. She hadn't set out to be the leader of this coven, but that's what she'd become. These girls were her family, and they needed her to push them to the finish line.

"We have Farrow's body, and there's still blood in her veins." It was a morbid thought, but using Farrow's blood was still their only option.

"What exactly are you suggesting?" Faith asked in a hushed voice.

Her cousin had stopped rocking, but she still looked shell-shocked.

Haven knew today was the worst day of Faith's life, so she tried to be gentle as she explained. "I'm suggesting that we give your mother exactly what she wanted. Let's put her body in the center of the clearing and give her to The Void."

Faith stared at her mother's burnt remains with a mix of shock and disgust on her face.

Reaching out, Haven placed a comforting hand on her arm. "She's gone, Faith, but we can still save Fallon if we act quickly."

Fallon shuddered, and the rain came in response to her pain.

"It's okay, Mom, just hold on," Phoebe begged.

Staring up at the sky, she felt a sense of trepidation. The rain was going to be a problem, and she wasn't sure if Fallon had the power to control it in her current state.

"Faith, can you help Phoebe get Fallon over to the clearing?"

"Sarin, help me with Farrow."

Asking Faith to carry her mother's dead body would be too much right now, and the fact that the girl didn't protest spoke volumes.

The ground quaked as they carried Farrow's body to the clearing. The smell of burnt flesh threatened to make her gag, but she fought the urge for Faith's sake. Lighting struck inside the clearing, and Haven knew The Void was making itself known.

Laying Farrow's body on the ground just outside the clearing, Haven offered the athame to Faith. "Do you want to do it? If you can't, I got you."

She wasn't sure if Faith had the strength to do what needed to be done but giving her the choice was the right thing to do.

"It should be me," Faith answered as she took the knife from Haven's hand.

Tears streamed down Faith's face as she picked up her mother's lifeless arm and sliced the knife across her wrist. Scrambling, Haven managed to slide a bowl underneath Farrow's arm as the blood rushed out.

Lightning struck again, right next to Haven's foot. "Take your places! It's now or never!"

The girls crawled to their respective places as the earth inside the clearing rose and fell with the angry breath of The Void. Then, the dirt fell away completely to reveal the beast lying in wait. The Void was a black chasm of nothingness, the perfect depiction of its name. The swirling portal undulated and expanded before contracting back in on itself over and over again. They didn't need her blood for the next part, but they were in this together. Scooting closer to Sarin, Haven urged her cousin to draw her sigil for spirit. Fallon was propped up against a log, and when Sarin passed the knife her way, Phoebe took it and handed it to Faith instead. There was already so much blood coating Fallon that Phoebe didn't need to cut her to get what they needed. Taking her mother by the hand, Phoebe helped her trace the sigil for water before cutting her own hand to complete the sigil for air. The rain washed away some of Phoebe's blood, forcing her to repeat the process, and if this kept up, they would never complete the symbols in time.

"Fallon, can you stop the rain?" Haven asked in a hushed plea.

Looking up to the sky, the strain on Fallon's face was palpable as she tried to activate her power. The rain slowed but didn't stop.

"I'll hold it as long as I can," Fallon promised in a pained voice.

Motioning for Faith to use the knife, Haven watched as her cousin drew the symbol for fire before dipping her finger into the bowl of Farrow's blood to complete the symbol for earth. Taking the knife from Faith, she sliced her own hand right over Lucifer's brand, hoping the magic in her blood would help fuel the spell, and just as before, the sigils lit up with a bright, glowing white light. They were too spread out to join hands, but their voices rose together as they chanted the words to the spell Haven's mother had given them.

Haven led them through the spell three times, but when she opened her eyes, nothing had changed. The Void still swirled in a turbulent abyss before them. She urged the girls to repeat the words to the spell, but it was no use. The light in the sigils dimmed before blinking out completely.

"Why isn't it working?" Faith yelled from her position across the clearing. Fallon met her worried stare with one of her own.

"I think I might know," Fallon groaned as she tried to sit up. "When my sister died, I don't think she was a witch anymore. If her transformation into a Dryad was complete, then her blood can't help us."

The darkness inside The Void began to spill out as if it knew it had already won. Its inky tendrils wrapped themselves around Farrow's body and pulled it into the clearing. Faith reached for her mother, but it was too late. Consumed by the swirling darkness of The Void, Farrow's body was reclaimed by the very thing that had created it.

"What do we do now?" Sarin asked with a panicked cry.

For once, Haven had no idea. "Give me a second. I'm thinking."

The hair on her arms stood on end as lightning struck the center of The Void itself. Opening her palm, she stared at the brand Lucifer had given her. This was their last hope. He was their last hope. Peering at the raised skin that represented their bond, she willed his power to come to the surface.

Sarin grabbed her by the hand, unaware of what she was trying to do. "It's okay, Haven. You got us this far!"

Haven's head shot back as the enormity of Lucifer's power filled her body. The vision was crystal clear, and in that moment, she finally saw Sarin for what she truly was. Standing in a sundrenched field with both palms outstretched, Sarin balanced a shifting tide of symbols. Fire, Earth, Air, Water, and Spirit, were all there inside Sarin's hands. Behind her, a swarm of locusts devoured a field full of decaying plants so new growth could begin. This was what Haven's dream about the locusts had been trying to tell her. This revelation was what her magic, tainted by The Void, hadn't been able to sense in Sarin. Lucifer's power showed her the truth. Sarin was rarest of all witch kind. She was a mimic. A powerful witch who could wield any element. The locusts had been a sign that Sarin held the power to transform. Sarin was the answer.

As the vision faded, Haven opened her eyes and stared at her cousin with a sense of wonder. "It was always you, Sarin."

"What are you talking about?" Sarin asked in an uneven tone.

"I saw you, Sarin. There's always been something inside of you that I couldn't explain, but Lucifer's power showed me the truth. You have the power to mimic. Faith, toss me the knife."

Faith threw the knife across the clearing, and Haven held her breath as the inky tendrils of The Void raced up to try and intercept it.

"No!" Phoebe screamed.

Using her air magic, the teen pushed a massive gust of wind through the clearing that knocked the knife out of The Void's reach. It spun through the air, hilt over blade, before landing in a muddy puddle beside Sarin.

"You can stand in for Farrow, Sarin. Draw the symbol for earth. Do it now!" Haven demanded as her palms began to sweat.

The Void's tendrils emerged again, and this time, it had one aimed at each of them. Haven shot a ball of fire at the one closest to her, and a chilling shriek rang out as it retreated back to The Void.

Haven felt Sarin's hesitation, but they were out of time. Her cousin needed to act now. "I know this is hard to understand, Sarin, but if you trust me, I need you to do this!"

"I do trust you!" Sarin declared as she squeezed the open wound on her hand and drew the sigil for earth in a hurried frenzy.

Grabbing onto Sarin's hand, she prompted the girls to call out the words to the spell once more as The Void's foot soldiers slithered closer to them. Sarin, Faith, Phoebe, and Fallon joined her until the cacophony of their voices reached a fever pitch. The wind whipped up a dozen small tornadoes that danced around the five of them like shadows as the magic in their voices blended into a sweet symphony of power. The sky dimmed and flickered as the earth reclaimed the magic it was owed, and the balance of nature was restored.

A horrible screeching sound echoed from inside The Void as it began to close in on itself in a rush of blackness. As the darkness retreated, Farrow's body came back into view. Her remains were floating in the middle of the chaos, and to everyone's shock and dismay, her lifeless body sat up in a series of stiff, choppy movements as if it were being puppeted. Her midnight-colored eyes reflected nothing but death and despair, and Haven knew The Void was using her body to make its final stand. The Void used Farrow's burnt and disfigured face to assess each one of them, before opening its borrowed lips on a vicious hiss. It was the most horrific sight Haven had ever witnessed. Lurching to the side, the empty husk that had once been Farrow grabbed hold of Fallon and pulled her inside of the clearing, right into the heart of The Void. Phoebe screamed as her mother was ripped from her arms.

"You took one from me. Now, I take one from you!" The Void taunted through Farrow's blackened lips.

Phoebe reached for her mother, but Faith pulled her back just in time.

"I love you, Phoebe! Never forget that!" Fallon cried as The Void closed in on itself, taking her with it.

The ground began to settle as The Void disappeared completely, leaving only a charred ring of dirt in its wake. Phoebe crawled into the clearing and started frantically digging in the dirt as if that would bring her mother back. It was heartbreaking to watch.

Faith got to Phoebe first, and as she gently stroked the teen's hair, Haven wept over what The Void had stolen from them. They'd won, even though it didn't feel like it, and as she embraced Sarin, they stayed back to give Phoebe and Faith the space they needed.

"Haven?" A familiar voice called out from behind her.

Turning, Haven was shocked to see her mother standing near the woods, and she wasn't alone. An older man was with her, a man who looked so similar to her mother that there was no denying their relation. Haven wanted to run to her mother, but the reality of the situation made her pause. Was this real, or just some last fuck you trick from The Void? Could her mother really be here, in this time and place? Had closing The Void destroyed the pocket realm along with it? She wasn't sure of anything, but her heart wanted to believe it was real. Her mother moved first, and when she pulled Haven into her arms, all her doubts were erased.

Pulling herself out of her mother's embrace, Haven stared at the man who was still standing back, looking scared and uncomfortable. "Who is that?"

Her mother smiled, and the warmth inside it threatened to burst her heart wide open. "That's my brother, Holden. The Void took him too, years before me."

Haven saw Sarin turn white as a sheet as Holden took a step toward them.

"Dad?" Sarin asked in a tentative voice.

Holden nodded as he stared back at Sarin with a look of longing in his eyes.

The journey to get here had been a long one, filled with a mountain of grief and heartache. But as Haven looked at her mother's loving face and the faces of her newfound family, she felt like the universe had finally given her a win. The road to recovery was going to be a long one, but she was ready to embrace it with all its beauty and sorrow. With her mother and her coven by her side, there was nothing they couldn't overcome.

The End

EPILOGUE

A few weeks later...

HAVEN

Haven couldn't contain her happiness as she sat across from her parents at the dining room table. She'd dreamt of a day like this for most of her life, and now that it was here, the moment felt surreal. Before leaving Canada, she'd called her dad to tell him the mind-blowing news, and it had taken a lot of coaxing and arguing to get him to stay put while she and her mother traveled back to Colorado. Flying with someone who had no identification was a big no-go, so when Faith offered to let her use Farrow's car indefinitely, Haven had been more than willing to accept the gift. The car she'd used during her time in Canada had been left at the cabin for the owner to reclaim. Saying goodbye to the girls had been a real tearjerker moment, but Haven needed to get back home to sort out life with her mother. Sarin was trying her best to navigate her new situation as well. Finding her dad had been a happy distraction, but she knew the grief over losing her mother was still brimming under the surface. Phoebe had been inconsolable after losing her mother and twin sister in a matter of weeks, and thankfully, Faith had stepped up to help. They were going to counseling together, and Faith had taken on more of a motherly role to her younger cousin. Faith was doing okay, depending on the day, and with Farrow gone, her dad had finally snapped out of his magic-fueled haze. She hoped the two of them could make up for lost time, and he could offer her some support while she took care of Phoebe. Haven was thankful the girls had each other, even though the future was uncertain. When you went through a traumatic experience, it was hard to find people who really understood, and their shared losses had bonded them together in ways she could have never imagined. They were sisters in every sense of the word—sisters in magic and in grief, and she would always be there for them whenever they needed her.

The drive from Canada to Colorado had taken a few days, and Haven was grateful for the alone time with her mother. Her mom had been trapped inside The Nothing, as she'd coined it, for over a decade, and since she hadn't changed physically, they looked the same age. She was going to have to come up with a convincing story to try and explain who her mother was once they got reacclimated in town. Over the course of the trip, she'd been nervous about her parents' reunion. She knew her dad had never stopped loving her mother, but what if her mother didn't want him anymore? What if her mother's time in The Nothing had fundamentally changed her? Luckily, all those fears were erased the moment they pulled into the driveway. Her dad had come barreling out of the house like his life depended on it, and the moment her mother laid eyes on him, she'd jumped out of the car and into his waiting arms. They weren't being romantic just yet, but their love for each other was palpable, and only time would tell where their love story went from here.

She'd just excused herself from the dinner table when a feeling of unease washed over her. It was the same off-putting sensation she'd been having off and on since they left Canada. Her powers had returned to normal the moment they closed The Void, but she hadn't been feeling well the last few days. Maybe it was magical burnout from using Lucifer's power, or maybe she was coming down with something. The following morning, she woke up to a sick feeling in the pit of her stomach. Running into the hallway bathroom, she'd barely made it to the toilet before she threw up. Leaning half over the open bowl, she sat there dry, heaving until the intense churning inside her stomach finally passed.

"Still feeling bad?" her mother asked as she peeked her head inside the bathroom.

She responded with a pain-filled groan as the sickness threatened to return.

"Maybe you caught the flu? Here, let me feel your head."

The moment her mother touched her, she let out a sharp gasp.

"Why are you looking at me like that?" Haven asked as she swallowed down another wave of nausea.

Sinking to the tiled floor, her mother stared at her in silence.

"Mom, you're scaring me. Did you see something?"

"A child... I saw an extraordinary child."

"Okay? That's not a lot to go on. If you had a vision, can you tell me more about it? Are we supposed to help this child or something?"

Her mother shook her head as she pointed at Haven's stomach. "The child I saw is yours, Haven. You're pregnant, and your daughter is going to change the world."

Haven felt the world tilt under the weight of her mother's words. It all made sense now; she just hadn't understood it at the time. She and Lucifer had cast the spell to find the Antichrist right after they'd had sex, and the spell hadn't been able to reveal its identity or location because, technically, it hadn't been created yet. But now, she was pregnant with Lucifer's child. She was pregnant with the Antichrist.

LUCIFER

Lucifer woke to find himself covered in a cold sweat, which was strange since he lived in a place full of hellfire. He didn't need to sleep, but sometimes, closing off his mind was a sweet reprieve from the raging evil all around him. The dream had been a vision; he knew that without a doubt, but he didn't have visions. His celestial powers were vast but not all-encompassing, and he knew this new vision had something to do with his bond with Haven. He yearned to see her again, but after this latest turn of events, he wasn't sure if she would welcome him with open arms. He'd been honest when he'd told her that he only wished to be free of Hell, but now, with the pending arrival of the Antichrist and the particulars of how she'd been created, he wasn't sure if Haven still believed him.

The vision had been a glimpse of the future and what his infatuation with the witch had brought down upon them all. He'd known the moment he set eyes on Haven that they had a shared destiny, but he hadn't, for one second, considered this possibility. A picture of the young girl's face from the vision flashed inside his mind. She was beautiful and terrifying. A perfect mix of light and dark, with Haven's facial features and his blood-red eyes. In the vision, the girl stood motionless, with her legs straddling the sides of two possible realities; on her left sat a thriving land of paradise filled with peace and light, but on her right, a burning black wasteland was all that remained of this world. As her midnight hair blew in the nonexistent wind, she held a golden scale in the palm of her hand. The scale weighed the collective sins of man, and the heavy plight of those souls would sway her decision to save or destroy this world.

Blinking his way back to reality, Lucifer felt out of control for the first time in his very long existence. He'd wanted to find the Antichrist in order to be free of Hell, but now that he knew it was his daughter, he wasn't sure he could damn her to the same fate he'd been destined to live with for millennia. Would he even have a choice? If she had the power to save or shatter the entire world, then what sway could he possibly have over her? And in the meantime, how was he going to explain all of this to Haven? He'd had no idea he was even capable of fathering a child, let alone the Antichrist, and now, there was no going back. His daughter was coming, and only time would tell if she would usher in a new world of peace or destroy them all.

ABOUT THE AUTHOR

Angela Dunham was born and raised in Florida and has had a passion for creative writing since childhood. Her love of all things magic and macabre inspired her to write stories in which the two coexist.

Angela's books are a mix of fast-paced action and suspense, with underlying themes of found family and the transformative power of love. Angela's writing spans genres, with a focus on paranormal, urban fantasy, and horror. Angela writes complex and snarky characters that leave her readers coming back for more.

Angela is Halloween-obsessed and loves to tell stories about the things that go bump in the night. When Angela isn't writing, you can find her reading a good book, wrangling her adorable son, or drinking an iced chai tea latte.

ALSO BY